TURNED

(book #1 in the vampire journals)

Morgan Rice

ISBN: 978-1-939416-30-8

ACCLAIM FOR MORGAN RICE'S BOOKS

"Grabbed my attention from the beginning and did not let go....This story is an amazing adventure that is fast paced and action packed from the very beginning. There is not a dull moment to be found."
--Paranormal Romance Guild {regarding *Turned*}

"A great plot, and this especially was the kind of book you will have trouble putting down at night. The ending was a cliffhanger that was so spectacular that you will immediately want to buy the next book, just to see what happens."
--The Dallas Examiner{regarding *Loved*}

"A book to rival *Twilight* and *The Vampire Diaries*, and one that will have you wanting to keep reading until the very last page! If you are into adventure, love and vampires this book is the one for you!"
--vampirebooksite.com {regarding *Turned*}

"An ideal story for young readers. Morgan Rice did a good job spinning an interesting twist on what could have been a typical vampire tale. Refreshing and unique, has the classic elements found in many Young Adult paranormal stories."
--The Romance Reviews {regarding *Turned*}

"Rice does a great job of pulling you into the story from the beginning, utilizing a great descriptive quality that transcends the mere painting of the setting....Nicely written and an extremely fast read, this is a good start to a new vampire series sure to be a hit with readers who are looking for a light, yet entertaining story."
--Black Lagoon Reviews {regarding *Turned*}

"Jam packed with action, romance, adventure, and suspense. This book is a wonderful addition to this series and will have you wanting more from Morgan Rice."
--vampirebooksite.com {regarding *Loved*}

"Morgan Rice proves herself again to be an extremely talented storyteller....This would appeal to a wide range of audiences, including younger fans of the vampire/fantasy genre. It ended with an unexpected cliffhanger that leaves you shocked."
--The Romance Reviews {regarding *Loved*}

"Is it physical
To walk unbraced and suck up the humors
Of the dank morning? What, is Brutus sick,
And will he steal out of his wholesome bed
To dare the vile contagion of the night?"

--William Shakespeare, *Julius Caesar*

One

Caitlin Paine always dreaded her first day at a new school. There were the big things, like meeting new friends, the new teachers, learning new hallways. And there were the small things, like getting a new locker, the smell of a new place, the sounds it made. More than anything, she dreaded the stares. She felt that everyone in a new place always stared at her. All she wanted was anonymity. But it never seemed meant to be.

Caitlin couldn't understand why she was so conspicuous. At five foot five she wasn't especially tall, and with her brown hair and brown eyes (and normal weight) she felt she was average. Certainly not beautiful, like some of the other girls. At 18, she was a bit older, but not enough to make her stand out.

There was something else. There was something about her that made people look twice. She knew, deep down, that she was different. But she wasn't exactly sure how.

If there was anything worse than a first day, it was starting in midterm, after everyone already had time to bond. Today, this first day, in mid-March, was going to be one of the worst. She could feel it already.

In her wildest imagination, though, she never thought it would be *this* bad. Nothing she had ever seen—and she had seen a lot—had prepared her for this.

Caitlin stood outside her new school, a vast New York City public school, in the freezing March morning, and wondered, *Why me?* She was way underdressed, in just a sweater and leggings, and not even remotely prepared for the noisy chaos that greeted her.

Hundreds of kids stood there, clamoring, screaming, and shoving each other. It looked like a prison yard.

It was all too loud. These kids laughed too loud, cursed too much, shoved each other too hard. She would have thought it was a massive brawl if she didn't spot some smiles and mocking laughter. They just had too much energy, and she, exhausted, freezing, sleep-deprived, couldn't understand where it came from. She closed her eyes and wished it would all go away.

She reached into her pockets and felt something: her ipod. *Yes.* She put her headphones in her ears and turned it up. She needed to drown it all out.

But nothing came. She looked down and saw the battery was dead. *Perfect.*

She checked her phone, hoping for some distraction, anything. *No new messages.*

She looked up. Looking out at the sea of new faces, she felt alone. Not because she was the only white girl—she actually preferred that. Some of her closest friends at other schools had been black, Spanish, Asian, Indian—and some of her meanest frenemies had been white. No, that wasn't it. She felt alone because it was urban. She stood on concrete. A loud buzzer had rang to admit her into this "recreational area," and she had had to pass through large, metal gates. Now she was boxed in—caged in by massive metal gates, topped by barbed-wire. She felt like she'd gone to prison.

Looking up at the massive school, bars and cages on all the windows, didn't make her feel any better. She always adapted to new schools easily, large and small—but they had all been in suburbia. They had all had grass, trees, sky. Here, there was nothing but city. She felt like she couldn't breathe. It terrified her.

Another loud buzzer sounded and she shuffled her way, with hundreds of kids, towards the entrance. She was jostled roughly by a large girl, and dropped her journal. She picked it up (messing up her hair), and then looked up to see if the girl would apologize. But she was nowhere to be seen, having already moved on in the swarm. She did hear laughter, but couldn't tell if it was directed at her.

She clutched her journal, the one thing that grounded her. It had been with her everywhere. She kept notes and drawings in every place she went. It was a roadmap of her childhood.

She finally reached the entrance, and had to squeeze in just to walk through. It was like entering a train at rush hour. She had hoped it would be warm once she got inside, but the open doors behind her kept a stiff breeze blowing down her back, making the cold even worse.

Two large security guards stood at the entrance, flanked by two New York City policemen, in full uniform, guns conspicuously at their side.

"KEEP MOVING!" commanded one of them.

She couldn't fathom why two armed policemen would have to guard a high school entrance. Her feeling of dread grew. It got much worse when she looked up and saw that she'd have to pass through a metal detector with airport-style security.

Four more armed policemen stood on either side of the detector, along with two more security guards.

"EMPTY YOUR POCKETS!" snapped a guard.

Caitlin noticed the other kids filling small plastic containers with items from their pockets. She quickly did the same, inserting her ipod, wallet, keys.

She shuffled through the detector, and the alarm shrieked.

"YOU!" snapped a guard. "Off to the side!"

Of course.

All the kids stared as she was made to raise her arms, and the guard ran the handheld scanner up and down her body.

"Are you wearing any jewelry?"

She felt her wrists, then her neckline, and suddenly remembered. Her cross.

"Take it off," snapped the guard.

It was the necklace her grandmother gave her before she passed, a small, silver cross, engraved with a description in Latin which she never had translated. Her grandmother told her it was passed down by her grandmother. Caitlin wasn't religious, and didn't really understand what it all meant, but she knew it was hundreds of years old, and it was by far the most valuable thing she owned.

Caitlin lifted it from her shirt, holding it up, but not taking it off.

"I'd rather not," she answered.

The guard stared at her, cold as ice.

Suddenly, a commotion broke out. There was shouting as a cop grabbed a tall, thin kid and shoved him against a wall, removing a small knife from his pocket.

The guard went to assist, and Caitlin took the opportunity to slip into the crowd moving its way down the hall.

Welcome to New York public school, Caitlin thought. *Great.*

She was already counting the days to graduation.

*

The hallways were the widest she'd ever seen. She couldn't imagine that they could ever be filled, yet somehow they were completely packed, with all the kids crammed in shoulder to shoulder. There must have been thousands of kids in these halls, the sea of faces stretching endlessly. The noise in here was even worse, bouncing off the walls, condensed. She wanted to cover her ears. But she didn't even have elbow space to raise her arms. She felt claustrophobic.

The bell rang, and the energy increased.

Already late.

She scanned her room card again and finally spotted the room in the distance. She tried to cut across the sea of bodies, but wasn't getting anywhere. Finally, after several attempts, she realized she just had to get aggressive. She started elbowing and jostling back. One body at a time, she cut through all the kids, across the wide hall, and pushed the heavy door open to her classroom.

She braced herself for all the looks as she, the new girl, walked in late. She imagined the teacher scolding her for interrupting a silent room. But she was shocked to discover that was not the case at all. This room, designed for 30 kids but holding 50, was packed. Some kids sat in their seats, and others walked the aisles, shouting and yelling at each other. It was mayhem.

The bell had rang five full minutes ago, yet the teacher, disheveled, wearing a rumpled suit, hadn't even started the class. He actually sat with his feet up on the desk, reading the paper, ignoring everyone.

Caitlin walked over to him and placed her new I.D. card on the desk. She stood there and waited for him to look up, but he never did.

She finally cleared her throat.

"Excuse me."

He reluctantly lowered his newspaper.

"I'm Caitlin Paine. I'm new. I think I'm supposed to give you this."

"I'm just a sub," he replied, and raised his paper, blocking her.

She stood there, confused.

"So," she asked, "....you don't take attendance?"

"Your teacher's back on Monday," he snapped. "He'll deal with it."

Realizing the conversation was over, Caitlin took back her I.D. card.

She turned and faced the room. The mayhem hadn't stopped. If there was any saving grace, at least she wasn't conspicuous. No one here seemed to care about her, or to even notice her at all.

On the other hand, scanning the packed room was nerve-wracking: there didn't seem like any place left to sit.

She steeled herself and, clutching her journal, walked tentatively down one of the aisles, flinching a few times as she walked between unruly kids screaming at each other. As she reached the back, she could finally see the entire room.

Not one empty seat.

She stood there, feeling like an idiot, and felt other kids starting to notice her. She didn't know what to do. She certainly wasn't going to stand there the entire period, and the substitute teacher didn't seem to care either way. She turned and looked again, scanning helplessly.

She heard laughter from a few aisles away, and felt sure it was directed at her. She didn't dress like these kids did, and she didn't look like them. Her cheeks flushed as she started to feel really conspicuous.

Just as she was getting ready to walk out of the class, and maybe even out of this school, she heard a voice.

"Here."

She turned.

In the last row, beside the window, a tall boy stood from his desk.

"Sit," he said. "Please."

The room quieted a bit as the others waited to see how she'd react.

She walked up to him. She tried not to look up into his eyes— large, glowing green eyes—but she couldn't help it.

He was gorgeous. He had smooth, olive skin—she couldn't tell if he was Black, Spanish, White, or some combination—but she had never seen such smooth and soft skin, complimenting a chiseled jaw line. His hair was short and brown, and he was thin. There was something about him, something so out of place here. He seemed fragile. An artist, maybe.

It was unlike her to be smitten by a guy. She'd seen her friends have crushes, but she'd never really understood. Until now.

"Where will *you* sit?" she asked.

She tried to control her voice, but it didn't sound convincing. She hoped he couldn't hear how nervous she was.

He smiled wide, revealing perfect teeth.

"Right over here," he said, and moved to the large window sill, just a few feet away.

She looked at him, and he returned her stare, their eyes fully locking. She told herself to look away, but she couldn't.

"Thanks," she said, and was instantly mad at herself.

Thanks? That's all you could manage? Thanks!?

"That's right, Barack!" yelled a voice. "Give that nice white girl your seat!"

Laughter followed, and the noise in the room suddenly picked up again, as everyone ignored them once again.

Caitlin saw him lower his head, embarrassed.

"Barack?" she asked. "Is that your name?"

"No," he answered, reddening. "That's just what they call me. As in Obama. They think I look like him."

She looked closely and realized that he *did* look like him.

"It's because I'm half black, part white, and part Puerto Rican."

"Well, I think that's a compliment," she said.

"Not the way *they* say it," he answered.

She observed him as he sat on the window sill, his confidence deflated, and she could tell that he was sensitive. Vulnerable, even. He didn't belong in this group of kids. It was crazy, but she almost felt protective of him.

"I'm Caitlin," she said, reaching out her hand and looking him in the eye.

He looked up, surprised, and his smile returned.

"Jonah," he answered.

He shook her hand firmly. A tingling sensation ran up her arm as she felt his smooth skin envelop her hand. She felt like she melted into him. He held her grip a second too long, and she couldn't help smiling back.

*

The rest of the morning was a blur, and Caitlin was hungry by the time she reached the cafeteria. She opened the double doors and was taken aback by the enormous room, the incredible noise of what seemed like a thousand kids, all screaming. It was like entering a gymnasium. Except that every twenty feet there stood another security guard, in the aisles, watching carefully.

As usual, she had no idea where to go. She searched the huge room, and finally found a stack of trays. She took one, and entered what she thought was the food line.

"Don't you cut me, bitch!"

Caitlin turned and saw a large, overweight girl, half a foot taller than her, scowling down.

"I'm sorry, I didn't know—"

"Line's back there!" snapped another girl, pointing with her thumb.

Caitlin looked and saw that the line stretched back at least a hundred kids. It looked like a twenty minute wait.

As she started heading to the back of the line, a kid on the line shoved another one, and he went flying in front of her, hitting the ground hard.

The first kid jumped on top of the other and started punching him in the face.

The cafeteria erupted in a roar of excitement, as dozens of kids gathered around.

"FIGHT! FIGHT!"

Caitlin took several steps back, watching in horror at the violent scene at her feet.

Four security guards finally came over and broke it up, separating the two bloody kids and carting them off. They didn't seem to be in any hurry.

After Caitlin finally got her food, she scanned the room, hoping for a sign of Jonah. But he was nowhere in sight.

She walked down the aisles, passing table after table, all packed with kids. There were few free seats, and the ones that were free didn't seem that inviting, adjacent to large cliques of friends.

Finally, she took a seat at an empty table towards the back. There was just one kid at the far end of it, a short, frail Chinese boy with braces, poorly dressed, who kept his head lowered and focused on his food.

She felt alone. She looked down and checked her phone. There were a few Facebook messages from her friends from her last town. They wanted to know how she liked her new place. Somehow, she didn't feel like answering. They felt so far away.

Caitlin barely ate, a vague feeling of first-day nausea still with her. She tried to change her train of thought. She closed her eyes. She thought of her new apartment, a fifth floor walkup in a filthy building on 132nd street. Her nausea worsened. She breathed deeply, willing herself to focus on something, anything good in her life.

Her little brother. Sam. 14 going on 20. Sam never seemed to remember that he was the youngest: he always acted like her older brother. He'd grown tough and hardened from all the moving around, from their Dad's leaving, from the way their Mom treated them both. She could see it was getting to him and could see that he was starting to close himself off. His frequent school fights didn't surprise her. She feared it would only get worse.

But when it came to Caitlin, Sam absolutely loved her. And she him. He was the only constant in her life, the only one she could rely on. He seemed to retain his one soft spot left in the world for her. She was determined to do her best to protect him.

"Caitlin?"

She jumped.

Standing over her, tray in one hand and violin case in the other, was Jonah.

"Mind if I join you?"

"Yes—I mean no," she said, flustered.

Idiot, she thought. *Stop acting so nervous.*

Jonah flashed that smile of his, then sat across from her. He sat erect, with perfect posture, and put his violin down carefully beside him. He gently laid out his food. There was something about him, something she couldn't quite place. He was different than anyone she'd ever met. It was like he was from a different era. He definitely did not belong in this place.

"How's your first day?" he asked.

"Not what I expected."

"I know what you mean," he said.

"Is that a violin?"

She nodded to his instrument. He kept it close, and kept one hand resting on it, as if afraid someone might steal it.

"It's a viola, actually. It's just a little bigger, but it's a much different sound. More mellow."

She'd never seen a viola, and hoped that he'd put it on the table and show her. But he didn't make a move to, and she didn't want to pry. He was still resting his hand on it, and he seemed protective of it, like it was personal and private.

"Do you practice a lot?"

Jonah shrugged. "A few hours a day," he said casually.

"A few *hours*!? You must be great!"

He shrugged again. "I'm OK, I guess. There are a lot of players much better than me. But I am hoping it's my ticket out of this place."

"I always wanted to play the piano," Caitlin said.

"Why don't you?"

She was going to say, *I never had one,* but stopped herself. Instead, she shrugged and looked back down at her food.

"You don't need to own a piano," Jonah said.

She looked up, startled that he'd read her mind.

"There's a rehearsal room in this school. For all the bad here, at least there's some good. They'll give you lessons for free. All you have to do is sign up."

Caitlin's eyes widened.

"Really?"

"There's a signup sheet outside the music room. Ask for Mrs. Lennox. Tell her you're my friend."

Friend. Caitlin liked the sound of that word. She slowly felt a happiness welling up inside of her.

She smiled wide. Their eyes locked for a moment.

Staring back into his glowing, green eyes, she burned with a desire to ask him a million questions: *Do you have a girlfriend? Why are you being so nice? Do you really like me?*

But, instead, she bit her tongue and said nothing.

Afraid that their time together would run out soon, she scanned her brain for something to ask him that would prolong their conversation. She tried to think of something that would assure her that she'd see him again. But she got nervous and froze up.

She finally opened her mouth, and just as she did, the bell rang.

The room erupted into noise and motion, and Jonah stood, grabbing his viola.

"I'm late," he said, gathering his tray.

He looked over at her tray. "Can I take yours?"

She looked down, realizing she'd forgotten it, and shook her head.

"OK," he said.

He stood there, suddenly shy, not knowing what to say.

"Well…see you."

"See you," she answered lamely, her voice barely above a whisper.

*

Her first school day over, Caitlin exited the building into the sunny, March afternoon. Although a strong breeze was blowing, she didn't feel cold anymore. Although all the kids around her were screaming as they streamed out, she was no longer bothered by the noise. She felt alive, and free. The rest of the day had gone by in a blur; she couldn't even remember the name of a single new teacher.

She could not stop thinking about Jonah.

She wondered if she had acted like an idiot in the cafeteria. She had stumbled over her words; she barely even asked him any questions. All she could think of to ask him was about that stupid viola. She should have asked where he lived, where he was from, where he was applying to college.

Most of all, if he had a girlfriend. Someone like him had to be dating someone.

Just at that moment, a pretty, well-dressed Hispanic girl brushed by Caitlin. Caitlin looked her up and down as she passed, and wondered for a second if it was her.

Caitlin turned down 134th street, and for a second, forgot where she was going. She'd never walked home from school before, and for a moment, she blanked on where her new apartment was. She stood there on the corner, disoriented. A cloud covered the sun and a strong wind picked up, and she suddenly felt cold again.

"Hey, *amiga*!"

Caitlin turned, and realized she was standing in front of a filthy, corner bodega. Four seedy men sat in plastic chairs before it, seemingly oblivious to the cold, grinning at her as if she were their next meal.

"Come over here, baby!" yelled another.

She remembered.

132nd street. That's it.

She quickly turned and walked at a brisk pace down another side street. She checked over her shoulder a few times to see if those men were following her. Luckily, they weren't.

The cold wind stung her cheeks and woke her up, as the harsh reality of her new neighborhood started to sink in. She looked around at the abandoned cars, the graffitied walls, the barbed-wire, the bars on all the windows, and she suddenly felt very alone. And very afraid.

It was only 3 more blocks to her apartment, but it felt like a lifetime away. She wished she had a friend at her side—even better, Jonah—and she wondered if she could manage this walk alone every day. Once again, she felt angry at her Mom. How could she keep moving her, keep putting her in new places that she hated? When would it ever end?

Broken glass.

Caitlin's heart beat faster as she saw some activity up on the left, on the other side of the street. She walked quickly and tried to keep her head down, but as she got closer, she heard yells and grotesque laughter, and she couldn't help but notice what was going on.

Four huge kids—18 or 19, maybe—stood standing over another kid. Two of them held his arms, while the third stepped in and punched him in the gut, and the fourth stepped up and punched him in the face. The kid, maybe 17, tall, thin and defenseless, fell to the ground. Two of the boys stepped up and kicked him in the face.

Despite herself, Caitlin stopped and stared. She was horrified. She had never seen anything like it.

The other two kids took a few steps around their victim, then raised their boots high and brought them down.

Caitlin was afraid they were going to stomp the kid to death.

"NO!" she screamed.

There was a sick crunching sound as they brought their feet down.

But it wasn't the sound of broken bone—rather, it was the sound of wood. Crunching wood. Caitlin saw that they were stomping a small, musical instrument. She looked closely, and saw bits and pieces of a viola all over the sidewalk.

She raised her hand to her mouth in horror.

"Jonah!?"

Without thinking, Caitlin crossed the street, right to the pack of guys, who had by now begun to notice her. They looked at her and their evil smiles broadened as they elbowed each other.

She walked right up to the victim and saw that it was indeed Jonah. His face was bleeding and bruised, and he was unconscious.

She looked up at the pack of kids, her anger overpowering her fear, and stood between Jonah and them.

"Leave him alone!" she shouted to the group.

The kid in the middle, at least six-four, muscular, laughed back.

"Or what?" he asked, his voice very deep.

Caitlin felt the world rush by her, and realized that she'd just been shoved hard from behind. She raised her elbows as she hit the concrete, but that barely cushioned her fall. Out of the corner of her eye, she could see her journal go flying, its loose papers spreading everywhere.

She heard laughter. And then footsteps, coming at her.

Heart pounding in her chest, her adrenaline kicked in. She managed to roll and scramble to her feet just before they reached her. She took off at a sprint down the alleyway, running for her life.

They followed close behind.

At one of her many schools, back when Caitlin thought she would have a long future somewhere, she took up Track, and realized she was good at it. The best on the team, actually. Not in long-distance, but in the 100 yard sprint. She could even outrun most of the guys. And now, it came flooding back to her.

She ran for her life, and the guys couldn't catch her.

Caitlin glanced back and saw how far behind they were, and felt optimistic that she could outrun them all. She just had to make the right turns.

The alleyway ended in a T, and she could either turn left or right. She wouldn't have time to change her decision if she wanted to maintain her lead, and she'd have to choose quick. She couldn't see what was around each corner, though. Blindly, she turned left.

She prayed it was the right choice. *Come on. Please!*

Her heart stopped as she made a sharp left and saw the dead end before her.

Wrong move.

A dead end. She ran right up to the wall, scanning for an exit, any exit. Realizing there was none, she turned to face her approaching attackers.

Out of breath, she watched them turn the corner and approach. She could see over their shoulders that if she had turned right, she would have been home free. Of course. Just her luck.

"All right, bitch," one of them said, "you're gonna suffer now."

Realizing she had no way out, they walked slowly towards her, breathing hard, grinning, and relishing the violence to come.

Caitlin closed her eyes and breathed deep. She tried to will Jonah to wake up, to appear around the corner, awake and all-powerful, ready to save her. But she opened her eyes and he wasn't there. Only her attackers. Getting closer.

She thought of her Mom, of how she hated her, of all the places she'd been forced to live. She thought of her brother Sam. She thought of what her life would be like after this day.

She thought of her whole life, of how she'd always been treated, of how no one understood her, of how nothing ever went her way. And something clicked. Somehow, she had had enough.

I don't deserve this. I DON'T deserve this!

And then, suddenly, she felt it.

It was a wave, something unlike anything she had ever experienced. It was a wave of rage, flooding through her, flushing her blood. It centered in her stomach, and spread from there. She could feel her feet rooted to the ground, as if she and the concrete were one, and could then feel a primal strength overcome her, course through her wrists, up her arms, into her shoulders.

Caitlin let out a primal roar that surprised and scared even her. As the first kid approached her and laid his beefy hand on her wrist, she watched as her hand reacted on its own, grabbing hold of her attacker's wrist and twisting it backwards at a right angle. The kid's face contorted in shock as his wrist, and then arm, were snapped in two.

He dropped to his knees, screaming.

The three other boys' eyes opened wide in surprise.

The largest of the three charged right at her.

"You fuc—"

Before he could finish, she had jumped up in the air and planted her two feet squarely in his chest, sending him flying back about ten feet and slamming into a stack of metal garbage cans.

He lay there, not moving.

The other two kids looked at each other, shocked. And truly scared.

Caitlin stepped up and, feeling an inhuman strength course through her, and heard herself snarl as she picked up the two kids (each twice her size), hoisting each several feet off the ground with a single hand.

As they hung dangling in the air, she swung them back, then swung them together, crushing each into the other with an incredible force. They both collapsed to the ground.

Caitlin stood there, breathing, foaming with rage.

All four boys were not moving.

She didn't feel relieved. On the contrary, she wanted more. More kids to fight. More bodies to throw.

And she wanted something else.

She suddenly had crystal clear vision, and was able to zoom in on their necks, exposed. She could see down to the tenth of an inch, and she could see, from where she stood, the veins pulsing in each. She wanted to bite. To feed.

Not understanding what was happening to her, she tossed her head back and let out an unearthly shriek, echoing off the buildings and down the block. It was a primal shriek of victory, and of unfulfilled rage.

It was the shriek of an animal that wanted more.

Two

Caitlin stood before the door to her new apartment, staring, and suddenly realized where she was. She had no idea how she got there. The last thing she remembered, she'd been in the alley. Somehow, she'd got herself back home.

She remembered, though, every second of what happened in that alleyway. She tried to erase it from her mind, but couldn't. She looked down at her arms and hands, expecting to see them look different—but they were normal. Just as they had always been. The rage had swept through her, transforming her, then had just as quickly left.

But the after-effects remained: she felt hollowed out, for one. Numb. And she felt something else. She couldn't quite figure it. Images kept flashing through her mind, images of those bullies' exposed necks. Of their heartbeat pulsing. And she felt a hunger. A craving.

Caitlin really didn't want to return home. She didn't want to deal with her Mom, especially today, didn't want to deal with a new place, with unpacking. If it weren't for Sam being in there, she may have just turned around and left. Where she'd go, she had no idea—but at least she'd be walking.

She took a deep breath and reached out and placed her hand on the knob. Either the knob was warm, or her hand was as cold as ice.

Caitlin entered the too-bright apartment. She could smell food on the stove—or probably, in the microwave. Sam. He always got home early and made himself dinner. Her Mom wouldn't be home for hours.

"That doesn't look like a good first day."

Caitlin turned, shocked at the sound of her Mom's voice. She sat there, on the couch, smoking a cigarette, already looking Caitlin up and down with scorn.

"What did ya, ruin that sweater already?"

Caitlin looked down and noticed for the first time the dirt stains; probably from hitting the cement.

"Why are you home so early?" Caitlin asked.

"First day for me, too, ya know," she snapped. "You're not the only one. Light workload. Boss sent me home early."

Caitlin couldn't take her Mom's nasty tone. Not tonight. She was always being snotty towards her, and tonight, Caitlin had enough. She decided to give her a taste of her own medicine.

"Great," Caitlin snapped back. "Does that mean we're moving again?"

Her Mom suddenly jumped to her feet. "You watch that fresh mouth of yours!" she screamed.

Caitlin knew her Mom had just been waiting for an excuse to yell at her. She figured it was best to just bait her and get it over with.

"You shouldn't smoke around Sam," Caitlin answered coldly, then entered her tiny bedroom and slammed the door behind her, locking it.

Immediately, her Mom banged at the door.

"You come out here, you little brat! What kind of way is that to talk to your mother!? Who puts bread on your table…."

On this night, Caitlin, so distracted, was able to drown out her Mom's voice. Instead, she replayed in her mind the day's events. The sound of those kids' laughter. The sound of her own heart pounding in her ears. The sound of her own roar.

What exactly had happened? How did she get such strength? Was it just an adrenaline rush? A part of her wished it was. But another part of her knew it wasn't. What was she?

The banging on her door continued, but Caitlin barely heard it. Her cell sat on her desk, vibrating like crazy, lighting up with IMs, texts, emails, Facebook chats—but she barely heard that, too.

She moved to her tiny window and looked down at the corner of Amsterdam Ave, and a new sound rose in her mind. It was the sound of Jonah's voice. The image of his smile. A low, deep, soothing voice. She recalled how delicate he was, how fragile he seemed. Then she saw him lying on the ground, bloody, his precious instrument in pieces. A fresh wave of anger arose.

Her anger morphed into worry—worry if he was all right, if he'd walked away, if he made it home. She imagined him calling to her. Caitlin. *Caitlin*.

"Caitlin?"

A new voice was outside her door. A boy's voice.

Confused, she snapped out of it.

"It's Sam. Let me in."

She went to her door and leaned her head against it.

"Mom's gone," said the voice on the other side. "Went down for cigarettes. Come on, let me in."

She opened the door.

Sam stood there, staring back, concern etched on his face. At 15, he looked older than his age. He'd grown early, to almost six feet, but he hadn't filled out yet, and he was awkward and gangly. With black hair and brown eyes, his coloring was similar to hers. They definitely looked related. She could see the concern on his face. He loved her more than anything.

She let him in, quickly closing the door behind him.

"Sorry," she said. "I just can't deal with her tonight."

"What happened with you two?"

"The usual. She was on me the second I walked in."

"I think she had a hard day," Sam said, trying to make peace between them, as always. "I hope they don't fire her again."

"Who cares? New York, Arizona, Texas…Who cares what's next? Our moving won't ever end."

Sam frowned as he sat on her desk chair, and she immediately felt bad. She sometimes had a harsh tongue, spoke without thinking, and she wished she could take it back.

"How was your first day?" she asked, trying to change the subject.

He shrugged. "OK, I guess." He toed the chair with his foot.

He looked up. "Yours?"

She shrugged. There must have been something in her expression, because he didn't look away. He kept looking at her.

"What happened?"

"Nothing," she said defensively, and turned and walked towards the window.

She could feel him watching her.

"You seem…different."

She paused, wondering if he knew, wondering if her outside appearance showed any changes. She swallowed.

"How?"

Silence.

"I don't know," he finally answered.

She stared out the window, watching aimlessly as a man outside the corner bodega slipped a buyer a dime bag.

"I hate this new place," he said.

She turned and faced him.

"So do I."

"I was even thinking about…" he lowered his head, "…taking off."

"What do you mean?"

He shrugged.

She looked at him. He seemed really depressed.

"Where?" she asked.

"Maybe…track down Dad."

"How? We have no idea where he is."

"I could try. I could find him."

"How?"

"I don't know…. But I could try."

"Sam. He could be dead for all we know."

"Don't say that!" he yelled, and his face turned bright red.

"Sorry," she said.

He calmed back down.

"But did you ever consider that, even if we found him, he may not even want to see us? After all, he left. And he's never tried to get in touch."

"Maybe cause Mom won't let him."

"Or maybe cause he just doesn't like us."

Sam's frown deepened as he toed the floor again. "I looked him up on Facebook."

Caitlin's eyes opened wide in surprise.

"You *found* him?"

"I'm not sure. There were 4 people with his name. 2 of them were private and had no picture. I sent them both a message."

"And?"

Sam shook his head.

"I haven't heard anything back."

"Dad would not be on Facebook."

"You don't know that," he answered, once again defensive.

Caitlin sighed and walked over to her bed and lay down. She stared up at the yellowing ceiling, paint peeling, and wondered how they all had reached this point. There were towns they'd been happy in, even times when their Mom seemed almost happy. Like when she was dating that guy. Happy enough, at least, to leave Caitlin alone.

There were towns, like the last one, where she and Sam both made a few good friends, where it seemed like they might actually stay—at least long enough to graduate in one place. And then it all seemed to turn so fast. Packing again. Saying goodbyes. Was it too much to ask for a normal childhood?

"I could move back to Oakville," Sam said suddenly, interrupting her thoughts. Their last town. It was uncanny how he always knew exactly what she was thinking. "I could stay with friends."

The day was getting to her. It was just too much. She wasn't thinking clearly, and in her frustration, what she was hearing was that Sam was getting ready to abandon her, too, that he didn't really care about her anymore.

"Then go!" she suddenly snapped, without meaning to. It was as if someone else had said it. She heard the harshness in her own voice, and immediately regretted it.

Why did she just have to blurt things out like that? Why couldn't she control herself?

If she'd been in a better mood, if she'd been calmer and hadn't had so much thrown at her at once, she wouldn't have said it. Or she would have been nicer. She would have said something like, *I know what you're trying to say is that you'd never leave this place, no matter how bad it got, because you wouldn't leave me alone to deal with all this. And I love you for it. And I'd never abandon you either. In this messed up childhood of ours, at least we have each other.* Instead, her mood had gotten the worst of her. Instead, she acted selfish, and snapped.

She sat up and could see the hurt etched on his face. She wanted to take it back, to say she was sorry, but she was just too overwhelmed. Somehow, she couldn't get herself to open her mouth.

In the silence, Sam slowly stood up from her desk chair and exited the room, gently closing the door behind him.

Idiot, she thought. *You're such an idiot. Why do you have to treat him the same way Mom treats you?*

She lay back down, staring at the ceiling. She realized that there was another reason she snapped. He'd interrupted her thoughts, and he'd done so just at a moment when they were turning for the worse. A dark thought had crossed her mind, and he'd cut her off before she'd had a chance to resolve it.

Her Mom 's ex-boyfriend. Three towns ago. It had been the one time her Mom had actually seemed happy. Frank. 50. Short, beefy, balding. Thick as a log. Smelled like cheap cologne. She had been 16.

She had been standing in the tiny laundry room, folding her clothes, when Frank appeared at the door. He was such a creep, always staring at her. He reached down and picked up a pair of her underwear, and she could feel her cheeks flush in embarrassment and anger. He held them up and grinned.

"Dropped these," he said, grinning. She'd snatched them out of his hands.

"What do you want?" she'd snapped back.

"Is that any way to talk to your new step-dad?"

He took a half step closer.

"You're not my step-dad."

"But I will be—soon."

She tried to go back to folding her clothes, but he took another step closer. Too close. Her heart pounded in her chest.

"I think it's time we got to know each other a little bit better," he'd said, removing his belt. "Don't you?"

Horrified, she tried to squeeze past him and out the door in the small room, but as she did, he blocked her way, and roughly grabbed her and slammed her back against the wall.

That's when it happened.

A rage had flooded through her. A rage unlike anything she'd ever experienced. She felt her body heating up, on fire, from her toes to her scalp. As he approached her, she jumped straight up and kicked him, planting both feet squarely on his chest.

Despite being a third of his size, he flew backwards through the door, cracking the wood off its hinges, and kept going, ten feet into the next room. It was as if a cannon had blasted him through the house.

Caitlin had stood there, trembling. She had never been a violent person, had never so much as punched someone. Moreover, she was not that big, or strong. How had she known had to kick him like that? How had she even had the strength to do it? She had never seen anyone—much less a grown man—go flying through the air, or shatter a door. Where had her strength come from?

She had walked over to him, and stood over him.

He was knocked out cold, flat on his back. She wondered if she'd killed him. But at that moment, the rage still filling her, she didn't really care. She was more worried about herself, about who—or what—she really was.

She never saw Frank again. He broke up with her Mom the next day, and never came back. Her Mom had suspected something happened between the two of them, but she never said a word. She did, though, blame Caitlin for the breakup, for ruining the one happy time in her life. And she hadn't stopped blaming her since.

Caitlin looked back up at her peeling ceiling, heart pounding all over again. She thought of today's rage, and wondered if the two episodes were connected. She had always assumed that Frank had just been a crazy, isolated incident, some weird burst of strength. But now she wondered if it was something more. Was there some kind of power inside of her? Was she some kind of freak?

Who was she?

Three

Caitlin ran. The bullies were back, and they were chasing her down the alleyway. A dead end lay before her, a massive wall, but she ran anyway, right towards it. As she ran, she picked up speed, impossible speed, and the buildings flew by in a blur. She could feel the wind rushing through her hair.

As she got closer, she leapt, and in a single bound she was at the top of the wall, thirty feet high. One more leap, and she flew through the air again, thirty feet, twenty, landing on the concrete without losing a stride, still running, running. She felt powerful, invincible. Her speed increased even more, and she felt like she could fly.

She looked down and before her eyes the concrete changed to grass—tall, swaying, green grass. She ran through a prairie, the sun shining, and she recognized it as the home of her early childhood.

In the distance, she could sense that her father stood on the horizon. As she ran, she felt she was getting closer to him. She saw him coming into focus. He stood with a large smile, and arms spread wide.

She ached to see him again. She ran for all she was worth. But as she got closer, he got further away.

Suddenly, she was falling.

A huge, medieval door opened, and she entered a church. She walked down a dimly-lit aisle, torches burning on either side of her. Before a pulpit, a man stood with his back to her, kneeling. As she got closer, he stood and turned.

It was a priest. He looked at her, and his face filled with fear. She felt the blood coursing through her veins, and she watched herself as she approached him, unable to stop herself. He raised a cross to her face, afraid.

She pounced on him. She felt her teeth grow long, too long, and watched as they plunged into the priest's neck.

He shrieked, but she didn't care. She felt his blood course through her teeth and into her veins, and it was the greatest feeling of her life.

Caitlin sat straight up in bed, breathing hard. She looked all around her, disoriented. Harsh morning sunlight streamed in.

Finally, she realized she had been dreaming. She wiped the cool sweat from her temples and sat on the edge of her bed.

Silence. Judging from the light, Sam and her Mom must have already left. She looked at the clock and saw that it was indeed late: 8:15. She'd be late for her second day of school.

Perfect.

She was surprised that Sam hadn't woken her up. In all their years, he'd never let her oversleep—he'd always wake her if he was leaving first.

He must still be mad about last night.

She glanced at her cell: dead. She had forgot to charge it. It was just as well. She didn't feel like talking to anyone.

She threw on some clothes from the floor and ran her hands through her hair. She normally would just leave without eating, but this morning she felt thirsty. Unusually thirsty. She went to the fridge and grabbed a half gallon of red grapefruit juice. In a sudden frenzy, she tore off the top and gulped it right from the container. She didn't stop gulping until she'd downed the entire half gallon.

She looked at the empty container. Had she just drank all of that? In her life, she'd never drank more than a half a glass. She watched herself reach up and crush the cardboard container in a single hand, down to a tiny ball. She couldn't understand what this newfound strength was that coursed through her veins. It was exciting. And scary.

She was still thirsty. And hungry. But not for food. Her veins screamed for something more, but she couldn't understand what.

*

It was strange to see the hallways of her school so empty, the complete opposite of the day before. With class in session, there wasn't a soul in site. She glanced at her watch: 8:40. There were 15 minutes left to her third class of the day. She wondered whether it was worth it to even go at all, but then again, she didn't know where else to go. So she followed the hallway numbers towards the room.

She stopped outside the classroom door, and could hear the teacher's voice. She hesitated. She hated to interrupt, to be so conspicuous. But she didn't see what other choice she had.

She took a deep breath and turned the metal knob.

She entered, and the entire class stopped and looked up at her. Including the teacher.

Silence.

"Ms...." the teacher, forgetting her name, walked to her desk and picked up a piece of paper, scanning it, "....Paine. The new girl. You are 25 minutes late."

A stern, older woman, the teacher glared down at Caitlin.

"What do you have to say for yourself?"

Caitlin hesitated.

"Sorry?"

"That's not good enough. It may be acceptable to be late to class wherever *you are* from, but it's certainly not acceptable here."

"Unacceptable," Caitlin said, and immediately regretted it.

An awkward silence covered the room.

"*Excuse* me?" the teacher asked, slowly.

"You said 'not acceptable.' You meant 'unacceptable.'"

"OH—SHIT!" exclaimed a noisy boy from the back of the room, and the entire class erupted into laughter.

The teacher's face turned bright red.

"You little brat. Report to the Principal's office right now!"

The teacher marched over and opened the door beside Caitlin. She stood inches away, close enough so that Caitlin could smell her cheap perfume. "Out of my classroom!"

Normally Caitlin would have slinked quietly out of the room—in fact, she would have never corrected a teacher to begin with. But something had shifted within her, something she didn't entirely understand, and she felt a defiance rising. She didn't feel that she had to show respect to anyone. And she no longer felt afraid.

Instead, Caitlin stood where she was, ignoring the teacher, and slowly scanned the classroom, looking for Jonah. The room was packed, and she looked row to row. No sign of him.

"Ms. Paine! Did you not hear what I said!?"

Caitlin looked defiantly back. Then she turned and slowly walked out of the room.

She could feel the door slam behind her, and then heard the muffled clamor in the room, followed by, "Quiet down, class!"

Caitlin continued down the empty hallway, wandering, not really sure where she was going.

She heard footsteps. In the distance, a security guard appeared. He walked right for her.

"Pass!" he barked at her, still a good twenty feet away.

"What?" she answered.

He got closer.

"Where's your hall pass? You're supposed to hold it out visibly at all times."

"What pass?"

He stopped and examined her. He was an ugly, mean-looking man, with a huge mole on his forehead.

"You can't walk the halls without a signed pass. You know that. Where is it?"

"I didn't know—"

He picked up his CB radio, and said into it, "Hall pass violation in wing 14. I'm bringing her to detention now."

"Detention?" Caitlin asked, confused. "What are you—"

He grabbed her roughly by the arm and yanked her down the hall.

"Not another word out of you!" he snapped.

Caitlin didn't like the feel of his fingers digging into her arm, leading her as if she were a child. She could feel the heat rising through her body. She felt the Rage coming on. She didn't quite know how, or why, but she knew. And she knew that, in moments, she wouldn't be able to control her anger—or her use of force.

She had to stop it before it was too late. She used every ounce of her will to make it stop. But as long as his fingers were on her, it would just not go away.

She flung her arm quickly, before the full power took over her, and watched as his hand went flying off of her, and as he stumbled several feet back.

He stared back at her, shocked that a girl her size could throw him several feet across the hall with just a slight jerk of her arm. He wavered between outrage and fear. She could see him debating whether to attack her or back off. He lowered his hand to his belt, on which hung a large can of pepper spray.

"Lay your hands on me again, young lady," he said in a cold rage, "and I will mace you."

"Then don't put your hands on me," she answered defiantly. She was shocked at the sound of her own voice. It had changed. It was deeper, more primal.

He slowly removed his hand from the spray. He gave in.

"Walk in front of me," he said. "Down the hall and up those stairs."

*

The security guard left her at the crowded entrance to the Principal's office, and as he did, his radio went off, and he hurried off to another location. Before he did, he turned to her.

"Don't let me see you in these hallways again," he snapped.

Caitlin turned and saw fifteen kids, all ages, sitting, standing, all apparently waiting to see the principal. They all seemed like misfits. They were being processed, one student at a time. A guard stood watch, but lackadaisically, nodding off as he stood.

Caitlin didn't feel like waiting half the day, and she certainly didn't feel like meeting the Principal. She shouldn't have been late to school, that's true, but she didn't deserve this. She'd had enough.

The hallway door opened and a security guard dragged in three more kids, fighting and shoving. Mayhem ensued in the small waiting area, which was completely packed. Then the bell rang, and beyond the glass doors, she could see the hallways filling up. It was now mayhem inside and out.

Caitlin saw her chance. As the door opened again, she ducked past another kid and slipped out into the hall.

She looked quickly over her shoulder, but didn't see anyone notice. She quickly cut across the thick crowd of kids, making it to the other side, then around the corner. She checked again: still no one coming.

She was safe. Even if the guards noticed her absence—which she doubted, since she was never even processed—she was already too far away to catch. She hurried even faster down the hall, putting more distance between them, and headed towards the cafeteria. She had to find Jonah. She had to know if he was all right.

The cafeteria was packed, and she quickly walked up and down the aisles, looking for him. Nothing. She walked a second time, slowly scanning every table, and still couldn't find him.

She regretted not going back to him, not checking on his wounds, not calling an ambulance. She wondered if he had been really hurt. Maybe he was in the hospital. Maybe he wouldn't even come back to school.

Depressed, she grabbed a tray of food and found a table with a clear view of the door. She sat there, hardly eating, and watched every kid who came in, hoping for a sign of him each time the door swung open.

But he never came.

The bell rang, and the cafeteria emptied out. Still, she sat there waiting.

Nothing.

*

The final bell of the school day rang, and Caitlin stood before her assigned locker. She looked down at the combination printed in the piece of paper in her hand, turned the knob and pulled. It didn't work. She looked down and tried the combination again. This time, it opened.

She stared at the empty, metal locker. The inside door was lined with graffiti. Otherwise, it was completely bare. Depressing. She thought of all her other schools, of how she would rush to find her locker, to open it, to memorize the combination, and to line the door with pictures of boys from magazines. It was her way of gaining a little bit of control, of making herself at home, of finding her one spot in the school, of making something familiar.

But somewhere along the line, a few schools ago, she became less enthusiastic. She began to wonder what the point was in even bothering, since it was only a matter of time until she had to move again. She became slower and slower to decorate her locker.

This time, she wouldn't even bother. She closed the door with a bang.

"Caitlin?"

She jumped.

Standing there, a foot away, stood Jonah.

He wore large sunglasses. She could see that the skin beneath them was swollen.

She was shocked to see him standing there. And thrilled. In fact, she was surprised at how thrilled she was. A warm, nervous feeling centered in her stomach. She felt her throat go dry.

There was so much she wanted to ask him: if he got home OK, if he saw those bullies again, if he saw her there…. But somehow, the words couldn't get themselves from her brain to her mouth.

"Hey," was all she managed to say.

He stood there, staring. He looked unsure how to begin.

"I missed you in class today," she said, and immediately regretted her choice of words.

Stupid. You should have said, "I didn't see you in class." "Miss" sounds desperate.

"I came in late," he said.

"Me, too," she said.

He shifted, looking uncomfortable. She noticed his viola was not at his side. So it was real. It wasn't all just a bad dream.

"Are you OK?" she asked.

She gestured at his glasses.

He reached up and slowly took them off.

His face was purple and swollen. There were cuts and bandages on his forehead and beside his eye.

"I've been better," he said. He seemed embarrassed.

"Oh my god," she said, feeling terrible at the sight. She knew she should at least feel good about having helped him, about sparing him more damage. But instead she felt bad for not being there sooner, for not coming back for him. But after…*it* had happened, it had all been a blur. She couldn't really remember how she'd even gotten home. "I'm so sorry."

"Did you hear how it happened?" he asked.

He looked at her intently, with his bright green eyes, and she felt he was testing her. As if he was trying to get her to admit that she was there.

Had he seen her? He couldn't have. He was out cold. Or was he? Did he maybe see what happened afterwards? Should she admit that she had been there?

On the one hand, she was dying to tell him how she had helped him, to win his approval, and his gratitude. On the other, there was no way she could explain what she did without seeming like either a liar or some kind of freak.

No, she concluded internally. *You can't tell him. You can't.*

"No," she lied. "I don't really know anyone here, remember?"

He paused.

"I got jumped," he said. "Walking home from school."

"I'm so sorry," she said again. She sounded like an idiot, repeating the same stupid phrase, but she didn't want to say anything that would give too much away.

"Yeah, my Dad's pretty pissed," he continued. "They got my viola."

"That sucks," she said. "Will he get you a new one?"

Jonah shook his head slowly. "He said no. He can't afford it. And that I should have been more careful with it."

Concern crossed Caitlin's face. "But I thought you said that was your ticket out?"

He shrugged.

"What will you do?" she asked.

"I don't know."

"Maybe the cops will find it," she said. She remembered, of course, that it was broken, but she thought that by saying this, it would help prove to him that she didn't know.

He looked her over carefully, as if trying to judge if she were lying.

Finally, he said, "They smashed it." He paused. "Some people just feel the need to destroy other peoples' stuff, I guess."

"Oh my god," she said, trying her best not to reveal anything, "that's horrible."

"My Dad's pissed at me that I didn't fight back….But that's not who I am."

"What jerks. Maybe the cops will catch them," she said.

A small grin passed Jonah's face. "That's the weird thing. They already got theirs."

"What do you mean?" she asked, trying to sound convincing.

"I found these guys down the alley, right after. They were beat down worse than me. Not even moving." His grin widened. "Someone got to them. I guess there is a God."

"That's so strange," she said.

"Maybe I have a guardian angel," he said, looking her over closely.

"Maybe," she answered.

He stared at her for a long time, as if waiting for her to volunteer something, to hint at something. But she didn't.

"And there was something even stranger than all that," he said, finally.

He reached down and pulled something out of his backpack, and held it out.

"I found this."

She stared down in shock. It was her journal.

She felt her cheeks redden as she took it, both delighted to have it back and horrified that he had this piece of evidence that she was there. He must know for sure now that she was lying.

"It has your name in it. It *is* yours, right?"

She nodded, surveying it. It was all there. She had forgotten about it.

"There were some loose pages. I gathered them all up and put them back in. I hope I got them all," he said.

"You did," she said softly, touched, embarrassed.

"I followed the trail of pages, and the funny thing is….they lead me down the alley."

She continued to look down at the book, refusing to make eye contact.

"How do you suppose your journal got there?" he asked.

She looked him in the eye, doing her best to keep a straight face.

"I was walking home last night, and I lost it somewhere. Maybe they found it."

He studied her.

Finally, he said, "Maybe."

They stood there, in silence.

"The weirdest thing of all," he continued, "is that, before I went completely unconscious, I could have sworn I saw you there, standing over me, yelling at those guys to leave me alone….Isn't that crazy?"

He studied her, and she looked him back, straight in the eye.

"I'd have to be pretty crazy to do a thing like that," she said. Despite herself, a small smile started at the corner of her mouth.

He paused, then broke into a wide grin.

"Yes," he answered, "you would."

Four

Caitlin was on cloud nine as she walked home from school, clutching her journal. She hadn't been this happy in she didn't know when. Jonah's words replayed in her head.

"There's this concert tonight. At Carnegie Hall. I've got two free tickets. They're the worst seats in the house, but the vocalist is supposed to be amazing."

"Are you asking me out?" she'd said, smiling.

He'd smiled back.

"If you don't mind going with this lump of bruises," he'd said, smiling back. *"After all, it is Friday night."*

She practically skipped home, unable to contain her excitement. She didn't know anything about classical music—she'd never even really listened to it before—but she didn't care. She'd go anywhere with him.

Carnegie Hall. He said the dress was fancy. What would she wear? She checked her watch. She wouldn't have much time to change if she was going to meet him at that café before the concert. She doubled her pace.

Before she knew it, she was home, and even the dreariness of her building didn't bring her down. She bounded up the five flights of stairs and hardly even felt it as she walked into her new apartment.

Her Mom's scream came right away: "You fucking bitch!"

Caitlin ducked just in time, as her Mom threw a book right at her face. It went flying past her, and smashed into the wall.

Before Caitlin could speak, her Mom charged—fingernails out, aiming right for her face.

Caitlin reached up and caught her wrists just in time. She tangled with her, going back and forth.

Caitlin could feel her newfound power surging through her veins, and she felt that she could throw her Mom across the room without even trying. But she willed herself to control it, and she shoved her off, but only hard enough to send her onto the couch.

Her Mom, on the couch, suddenly broke into tears. She sat there, sobbing.

"It's *your* fault!" she screamed between her sobs.

"What's *wrong* with you?" Caitlin screamed back, completely off guard, having no idea what was going on. Even for her Mom, this was crazy behavior.

"*Sam.*"

Her Mom held out a piece of notebook paper.

Caitlin's heart pounded as she took it, a feeling of dread washing over her. Whatever it was, she knew it couldn't be good.

"He's gone!"

Caitlin scanned the handwritten note. She couldn't really concentrate as she read, only picking out fragments—*running away...don't want to be here...back with my friends...don't try to find me.*

Her hands were shaking. Sam had done it. He'd really left. And he didn't even wait for her. Didn't even wait to say goodbye.

"It's because of *you!*" her Mom spat.

A part of Caitlin couldn't believe it. She ran through the apartment, opened Sam's door, half expecting to find him there.

But the room was empty. Immaculate. Not a single thing left. Sam had never kept his room that clean. It was true. He was really gone.

Caitlin felt the bile rise up in her throat. She couldn't help feeling that this time her Mom was right, that it *was* her fault. Sam had asked her. And she had said, "Just go."

Just go. Why did she have to say that? She planned on apologizing, on taking it back, the next morning, but he was already gone when she woke up. She was going to talk to him when she got home today. But now it was too late.

She knew where he must have gone. There's only one place he would go: their last town. He'd be OK. Better, probably, than he was here. He had friends there. The more it sank in, the less she worried. In fact, she was happy for him. He'd finally made it out. And she knew how to track him down.

But she'd have to deal with this later. She glanced at her watch and realized she was late. She ran into her room, quickly grabbed the nicest clothes and shoes she'd had, and threw them all in a gym bag. She'd have to go without makeup. There just wasn't time.

"Why do you have to destroy everything you touch!?" her Mom screamed, now right behind her. "I never should have taken you in!"

Caitlin stared back, shocked.

"What are you talking about!?"

"That's right," her Mom continued. "I took you in. You're not mine. You never were. You were *his*. You're not my real daughter. Do you hear me!? I'd be ashamed to have you as a daughter!"

Caitlin could see the venom in her black eyes. She'd never seen her Mom in this deep of a rage. Her eyes held murder.

"Why did you have to chase away the one thing that was good in my life!?" her Mom yelled.

This time her Mom charged her with two hands held out in front, and went right for her throat. Before Caitlin could react, she was being choked. Hard.

Caitlin fought for breath. But her Mom 's grip was iron. It was truly meant to kill.

The rage flooded Caitlin, and this time she couldn't stop it. She could feel the familiar, prickly heat, starting at her toes, and working its way up through her arms and shoulders. She let it envelop her. As it did, the muscles in her neck bulged. Without doing a thing, her Mom's grip loosened.

Her Mom must have seen the transformation begin, because she suddenly looked afraid. Caitlin threw her head back and roared. She had transformed into a thing of fear.

Her Mom dropped her grip, and took a step back and stared, mouth open.

Caitlin reached up with one hand and shoved her, and she went flying backwards with such force that she went through the wall, shattering it with a crash, and into the other room. She kept going, smashing into yet another wall, and collapsing, unconscious.

Caitlin breathed hard, trying to focus. She surveyed the apartment, asking herself if there was anything she wanted to take with her. She knew there was, but she couldn't think clearly. She grabbed her gym bag of clothes, and walked out of her room, through the rubble, past her mother.

Her Mom lay there, groaning, already starting to sit up.

Caitlin kept walking, right out of the apartment.

It was the last time, she vowed, she would see it again.

Five

Caitlin walked quickly in the cold, March night down the side street, her heart still pounding from her episode with her mother. The cold air stung her face, and it felt good. Calming. She breathed deeply, and felt free. She would never have to go back to that apartment again, never have to retrace those grimy steps. Never have to see this neighborhood. And never have to step foot in that school. She had no idea where she was going, but at least it would be far from here.

Caitlin reached the avenue and looked up, scanning for a free cab. After a minute or so of waiting, she realized she wouldn't get one. The subway was her only option.

Caitlin marched towards the 135th Street station. She'd never taken a New York City subway before. She wasn't really sure which line to take, or where to get off, and this was the worst time to experiment. She dreaded what she might encounter down in the station on a cold, March night—especially in this neighborhood.

She descended the graffiti-lined steps and approached the booth. Luckily, it was manned.

"I need to get to Columbus Circle," Caitlin said.

The overweight agent behind the plexiglass ignored her.

"Excuse me," Caitlin said, "but I need to –"

"I said down the platform!" snapped the woman.

"No you didn't," Caitlin answered. "You didn't say anything!"

The agent just ignored her again.

"How much is it?"

"Two fifty," snapped the agent.

Caitlin dug into her pocket and extracted three crumpled dollar bills. She slid them under the glass.

The agent, still ignoring her, slid back a Metrocard.

Caitlin just swiped the card and entered the system.

The platform was poorly lit, and nearly deserted. Two homeless people occupied the bench, draped in blankets. One slept, but the other looked up at her as she walked by. He started mumbling. Caitlin walked faster.

She went to the edge of the platform and leaned over, looking for the train. Nothing.

Come on. Come on.

She glanced at her watch yet again. Already five minutes late. She wondered how much longer it would take. She wondered if Jonah would leave. She couldn't blame him.

She noticed something moving quickly out of the corner of her eye. She turned. Nothing.

As she looked closely, she thought she saw a shadow creep along the white tiled, linoleum wall, then slink down into the railway track. She felt like she was being watched.

But she looked again and saw nothing.

I must be seeing things.

Caitlin walked over to the large subway map. It was scratched and torn and covered in graffiti, but she could still make out the subway line. At least she was at the right place. It should take her right to Columbus Circle. She started to feel a bit better.

"You lost, baby?"

Caitlin turned and saw a large, black man standing over her. He was unshaven, and when he grinned, she noticed that he was missing teeth. He leaned in too close, and she could smell his terrible breath. Drunk.

She sidestepped him and walked several feet away.

"Hey bitch, I'm talking to you!"

Caitlin kept walking.

The man seemed high, and he staggered and swayed as he slowly headed her way. But Caitlin walked much faster, and it was a long platform, so there was still room between them. She really wanted to avoid another confrontation. *Not here. Not now.*

He got closer. She wondered how long it would be until she'd have no choice but to confront him. *Please God, get me out of here.*

Just then, a deafening noise filled the station, and the train suddenly arrived. *Thank God.*

She boarded, and watched with satisfaction as the doors closed on the man. Drunk, he cursed and banged on the metal casing.

The train took off, and in moments he was no more than a blur. She was on her way out of this neighborhood. On her way to a new life.

*

Caitlin exited at Columbus Circle and walked at a brisk pace. She checked her watch again. She was 20 minutes late. She swallowed.

Please be there. Please don't go. Please.

As she walked, just a few blocks away, she suddenly felt a pang in her stomach. She stopped, taken aback by the intense pain.

She bent over, clutching her stomach, unable to move. She wondered if people were staring at her, but she was in too much pain to care. She'd never experienced anything like this before. She struggled to catch her breath.

People passed quickly by on either side, but no one stopped to check if she was OK.

After about a minute, she finally, slowly, stood back up. The pain began to subside.

She breathed deeply, wondering what it could possibly have been.

She began walking again, heading in the direction of the café. But she now felt completely disoriented. And something else….Hunger. It wasn't a normal hunger, but a deep, unquenchable thirst. As a woman walked past her, walking her dog, Caitlin noticed herself turning and staring at the animal. She found herself craning her neck and watching the animal as it walked past, and staring at its neck.

To her surprise, she could see the details of the veins on the dog's skin, the blood coursing through it. She watched the heartbeat through the blood, and she felt a dull, numbing sensation in her own teeth. She wanted that dog's blood.

As if sensing itself being watched, the dog turned as it walked, and stared with fear up at Caitlin. It growled, and hurried away. The owner of the dog turned and looked at Caitlin, not understanding.

Caitlin walked on. She couldn't understand what was happening to her. She loved dogs. She would never want to harm an animal, much less a fly. What was happening to her?

The hunger pains disappeared as quickly as they had come, and Caitlin felt herself returning to normal. As she rounded the corner, the café came into sight, and she doubled her pace, breathed deep, and almost felt herself again. She checked her watch. 30 minutes late. She prayed he'd be there.

She opened the doors. Her heart was pounding, this time not from pain, but from the fear that Jonah would be gone.

Caitlin quickly scanned the place. She walked in fast, out of breath, and already felt conspicuous. She could feel all eyes on her, and scanned the row of diners to her left, and to her right. But there was no sign of Jonah. Her heart fell. He must have left.

"Caitlin?"

Caitlin spun around. There, grinning, stood Jonah. She fell her heart swell with joy.

"I am so sorry," she said in a rush. "I am usually never late. I just — it just —"

"It's OK," he said, gently laying his hand on her shoulder. "Don't worry about it, really. I'm just glad you're okay," he added.

She looked up into his smiling, green eyes, framed by a still bruised and swollen face, and for the first time that day, she felt at peace. She felt that everything could be all right after all.

"The only thing is, we don't have much time if we're going to make it," he said. "We only have about five minutes. So I guess we'll have to have that cup of coffee another time."

"That's fine," she said. "I'm just so happy that we didn't miss the concert altogether. I feel like such a —"

Caitlin suddenly looked down and was horrified to realize that she was still dressed in her casual clothing. She was still clutching her gym bag which held her nice clothes and shoes. She had meant to get to the café early, slip into the bathroom, change into her nice clothing, and be ready to meet Jonah. Now she was standing there, facing him, dressed like a slob, and clutching a gym bag. Her cheeks reddened. She didn't know what to possibly say.

"Jonah, I am so sorry that I am dressed like this," she said. "I meant to change before I came, but….Did you say we have five minutes?"

He looked at his watch, a flash of concern crossing his face.

"Yes, but—"

"I'll be right back," she said, and before he could answer, she raced through the restaurant, heading for the bathroom.

Caitlin burst into the bathroom and locked it behind her. She tore open her gym bag and yanked out all of her nice clothing, now rumpled. She yanked off her clothes and sneakers, and quickly put on her black velvet skirt, and a white silk blouse. She also took out her faux diamond earrings and put them on. They were cheap, but they worked. She finished the outfit off with black, high-heeled shoes.

She checked the mirror. She was a little bit rumpled, not as bad as she would have imagined. Her slightly open blouse displayed the small, silver cross she still wore about her neck. She had no time for makeup, but at least she was dressed. She quickly ran her hands through the water and dabbed her hair, putting some strands in place. She completed the outfit with her black, leather clutch.

She was about to run out, when she noticed her pile of old clothing and sneakers. She hesitated, debating. She really didn't want to carry those clothes with her the rest of the night. In fact, she didn't ever want to wear those clothes again.

She picked them all up in a ball, and with great satisfaction crammed them into the garbage can in the corner of the room. She was now wearing her one and only outfit left in the world.

She felt good walking into her new life dressed like this.

Jonah waited for her outside the café, tapping his foot, glancing at his watch. When she opened the door, he spun, and when he saw her, all dressed up, he froze. He stared at her, speechless.

Caitlin had never seen a guy look at her that way before. She never really thought of herself as attractive. The way that Jonah looked at her made her feel...special. It made her feel, for the first time, like a woman.

"You...look beautiful," he said softly.

"Thanks," she said. *So do you*, she wanted to answer, but she held herself back.

With her newfound confidence, she walked up to him, slipped her hand into his arm, and gently lead the way towards Carnegie Hall. He walked with her, quickening the pace, placing his free hand on top of hers.

It felt good to be in a boy's arms. Despite everything that had happened that day, and the day before, Caitlin now felt as if she were walking on air.

Six

Carnegie Hall was absolutely packed. Jonah led the way as they fought through the thick crowd, towards Will Call. It was not easy getting there. It was a wealthy, demanding crowd, and everyone seemed like they were rushing to make the concert. She had never seen so many well-dressed people in one place. Most of the men were in black tie, and the women wore long evening gowns. Jewels glittered everywhere. It was exciting.

Jonah got the tickets and lead her up the stairs. He handed them to the usher, who tore them and handed back the stubs.

"Can I keep one?" Caitlin asked, as Jonah went to put the two ticket stubs in his pocket.

"Of course," he said, handing one to her.

She rubbed it with her thumb.

"I like hanging onto things like this," she added, blushing. "Sentimental, I guess."

Jonah smiled, as she stuck it in her front pocket.

They were directed by an usher down a luxurious hallway with thick, red carpeting. Framed pictures of artists and singers lined the walls.

"So, how did you score free tickets?" Caitlin asked.

"My viola teacher," he answered. "He has season tickets. He couldn't make it tonight, so he gave them to me. I hope it doesn't take away from it that I didn't pay for them myself," he added.

She looked at him, puzzled.

"Our date," he answered.

"Of course not," she said. "You brought me here. That's all that matters. This is awesome."

Caitlin and Jonah were directed by another usher into a small door, which opened up right into the concert hall. They were up high, maybe 50 feet, and in their small box area there were only 10 or 15 seats. Their seats were right on the edge of the balcony, flush against the railing.

Jonah opened the thick, plush chair for her, and she looked down at the massive crowd and at all of the performers. It was the classiest place she had ever been. She looked out at the sea of gray hair, and she felt 50 years too young to be here. But thrilled all the same.

Jonah sat, and their elbows touched, and she felt a thrill at the warmth of his body beside her. As they settled in and sat there, waiting, she wanted to reach over and take his hand, and hold it in hers. But she didn't want to risk being too bold. So she sat there, hoping that he would reach over and take hers. He didn't make any move. It was early. And maybe he was shy.

Instead, he pointed, leaning over the railing.

"The best violinists are seated closest to the lip of the stage," he said, pointing. "That woman there is one of the best in the world."

"Have you ever played here?" She asked.

Jonah laughed. "I wish," he said. "This hall is only 50 blocks away from us, but it might as well be a planet away in terms of talent. Maybe one day," he added.

She looked down at the stage, at the hundreds of performers tuning their instruments. They were all dressed in black tie, and they all seemed so serious, so focused. Against the back of the wall stood a huge choir.

Suddenly, a young man, maybe 20, with long, flowing black hair, dressed in a tux, strutted proudly onto the stage. He cut right through the aisle of performers, heading for the center. As he did, the entire audience rose to its feet and applauded.

"Who's he?" Caitlin asked.

He reached the center and bowed repeatedly, smiling. Even from up here, Caitlin see that he was startlingly attractive.

"Sergei Rakov," Jonah answered. "He's one of the best singers in the world."

"But he seems so young."

"It's not about age, but about talent," Jonah answered. "There is talent, and then there is *talent*. To get *that* kind of talent, you need to be born with it—and you *really* need to practice. Not four hours a day, but eight hours a day. Every day. I'd do it if I could, but my dad won't let me."

"Why not?"

"He doesn't want the viola to be the only thing in my life."

She could hear the disappointment in his voice.

Finally, the applause began to die down.

"They're playing Beethoven's Ninth Symphony tonight," Jonah said. "It's probably his most famous piece. Have you heard it before?"

Caitlin shook her head, feeling stupid. She'd had a classical music class back in ninth grade, but she'd barely listened to a word the teacher had said. She didn't really get it, and they had just moved, and her mind had been somewhere else. Now she wished she would have listened.

"It requires a huge orchestra," he said, "and a huge chorus. It probably demands more performers on stage than just about any other piece of music. It's exciting to watch. That's why this place is so packed."

She surveyed the room. There were thousands of people there. And not an empty seat.

"This symphony, it was Beethoven's last. He was dying, and he knew it. He put it to music. It's the sound of death coming." He turned to her and grinned, apologetically. "Sorry to be so morbid."

"No, that's OK," she said, and meant it. She loved hearing him talk. She loved the sound of his voice. She loved what he knew. All of her friends had the most frivolous conversations, and she wanted something more. She felt lucky to be with him.

There was so much she wanted to say to Jonah, so many questions she wanted to ask—but the lights suddenly dimmed and a hush came over the audience. It would have to wait. She leaned back and settled in.

She looked down and to her surprise, there was Jonah's hand. He placed it on the armrest between them, palm up, inviting hers. She reached over, slowly, so as not to seem too desperate, and placed her hand into his. His hand was soft and warm. She felt her hand melting into it.

As the orchestra began and the first notes played—soft, soothing, melodious notes—she felt a wave of bliss rushing over her, and realized that she'd never been so happy. She forgot all about the events of the day before. If this was the sound of death, she wanted to hear more.

*

As Caitlin sat there, getting lost in the music, wondering why she had never heard it before, wondering how long she could make her date with Jonah last, it happened again. The pain suddenly struck. It hit her in the gut, like it had on the street, and it took all of her willpower to keep herself from keeling over in front of Jonah. She gritted her teeth silently, and struggled to breathe. She could feel the sweat break out on her forehead.

Another pang.

This time she squealed out in pain, just a little bit, enough to barely be heard above the music, which was reaching a crescendo. Jonah must have heard, because he turned and looked at her, concerned. He gently placed a hand on her shoulder.

"Are you OK?" he asked.

She was not. Pain was overwhelming her. And something else: hunger. She felt absolutely ravenous. She had never been so overwhelmed by such a sensation in her life.

She glanced over at Jonah, and her eyes went straight for his neck. She fixated on the pulsing of his vein, tracked it as it went from his ear down towards his throat. She watched the throbbing. She counted the heartbeats.

"Caitlin?" he asked again.

The craving was overwhelming. She knew that if she sat there for even a second more, she would be unable to control herself. If left unrestrained, she would definitely sink her teeth into Jonah's neck.

With her last ounce of will, Caitlin suddenly bounded from her chair, climbing over Jonah in one swift leap, and racing up the stairs, for the door.

At that same moment, the lights in the room suddenly went on full blast, as the orchestra played its final note. Intermission. The entire audience leapt to its feet, clapping loudly.

Caitlin reached the exit door a few seconds before the masses could get out of their seats.

"Caitlin!?" Jonah yelled from somewhere behind her. He was probably getting out of his seat and following her.

She could not let him see her like this. More importantly, she could not allow him anywhere near her. She felt like an animal. She roved the empty hallways of Carnegie Hall, walking faster and faster, into she ran in a full-fledged sprint.

Before she knew it, she was running at impossible speed, tearing through the carpeted hallway. She was an animal on the hunt. She needed food. She knew enough to know that she had to get herself away from the masses. Fast.

She found an exit door and put her shoulder into it. It was locked, but she leaned into it with such force that it snapped off the hinges.

She found herself in a private stairwell. She raced down the steps, taking them three at a time, until she arrived at another door. She put her shoulder into that one too, and found herself in a new hallway.

This hallway was even more exclusive, and more empty, than the others. Even in her haze, she could tell that she had arrived in some sort of backstage area. She walked down the hallway, bending over in pain from the hunger, and knew that she could not last one second longer.

She raised her palm and shoved it into the first doorway she found, and it opened with one blow. It was a private dressing room.

Sitting before a mirror, admiring himself, was Sergei. The singer. This must be his backstage dressing area. Somehow, she had arrived back here.

He stood, annoyed.

"I am sorry, but no autographs right now," he snapped. "The security guards should have told you. This is my private time. Now, if you'll excuse me, I have to prepare."

With a guttural roar, Caitlin leapt right for his throat, sinking her teeth in deeply.

He screamed. But it was too late.

Her teeth sank deep into his veins. She drank. She felt his blood rushing through her veins, felt her craving begin to be satisfied. It was exactly what she'd needed. And she could not have waited a second more.

Sergei slumped, unconscious, into his chair, Caitlin leaned back, face covered in blood, and smiled. She had discovered a new taste. And nothing would stand in her way of it again.

Seven

New York Homicide detective Grace Grant opened the doors to Carnegie Hall and knew right away that it was going to be bad. She had seen the press out of control before, but never anything like this. Reporters were 10 deep, and unusually aggressive.

"Detective!"

They screamed for her repeatedly as she entered, the room filling with flashes.

As Grace and her detectives cut through the lobby, the reporters barely give an inch. At 40, muscular and hardened, with short black and hair and matching eyes, Grace was tough, and used to pushing her way through. But this time, it was not easy. The reporters knew it was a huge story, and they weren't going to give. This was going to make life much harder.

A young, international star murdered at the height of his fame and power. Right in the middle of Carnegie Hall and right in the middle of his American debut. The press had been here regardless, ready to cover the debut. Without even the slightest hiccup, the news of this performance was going to splash across the newspaper pages in every country in the world. If he had merely tripped, or fell, or sprained his ankle, the story would have been bumped up to Page 1.

And now this. Murdered. In the middle of his goddamn performance. Right in the hall where he sang just minutes before. It was just too much. The press had grabbed this one by the throat and they would not let it go.

Several reporters shoved microphones into her face.

"Detective Grant! There are reports that Sergei was killed by a wild animal. Is that true?"

She ignored them as she elbowed her way past.

"Why wasn't there better security inside of Carnegie Hall, detective?" asked another reporter.

Another reporter yelled, "There are reports that this was a serial killer. They're dubbing him the 'Beethoven Butcher.' Do you have any comment?"

As she reached the back of the room, she turned and faced them.

The crowd grew silent.

"Beethoven Butcher?" she repeated. "Can't they do better than that?"

Before they could ask another question, she abruptly exited the room.

Grace wound her way up the back staircase of Carnegie Hall, flanked by her detectives, who kept feeding her information as she went. The truth was, she was barely listening. She was tired. She had just turned 40 last week, and she knew she shouldn't be this tired. But the long, March nights had gotten to her, and she needed some rest. This was the third murder this month, not counting the suicides. She wanted warm weather, some greenery, some soft sand beneath her feet. She wanted a place where no one murdered anyone, where they didn't even think of suicide. She wanted a different life.

She checked her watch as she entered the corridor leading to backstage. 1 A.M.. Without having to look, she could already tell the crime scene was soiled. Why hadn't they called her here earlier?

She should have married, like her mother told her to, at 30. She'd had someone. He wasn't perfect, but he could have done. But she had held onto her career, like her father. It was what she thought her father wanted. Now her father was dead, and she never really found out what he wanted. And she was tired. And alone.

"No witnesses," snapped one of the detectives walking beside her. "Forensics say it happened sometime between 10:15 and 10:28 P.M. Not much signs of a struggle."

Grace didn't like this crime scene. There were way too many people involved, already and too many people had gotten here before her. Every move she made would be on display. And no matter what great investigative work she did, the credit would end up being stolen by someone else. There were just too many departments involved, which meant too much politics.

She finally brushed past the rest of the reporters, and entered the taped off area, reserved for only the elite officers. As she headed down the next hallway, things finally quieted down. She could think again.

The door to his dressing room stood slightly ajar. She reached up, donned a latex glove, and gently nudged it open the rest of the way.

She had seen it all in her 20 years as a cop. She'd seen people murdered in just about every possible way, even ways she could not have come up with in her worst nightmares. But she had never seen anything like this.

Not because it was particularly bloody. Not because some horrific violence had taken place. It was something else. Something surreal. It was too quiet. Everything was in perfect place. Except, of course, for the body. He sat slumped backwards in his chair, his neck exposed. And there, under the light, were two perfect holes, right in his jugular vein.

No blood. No signs of struggle. No torn clothing. Nothing else out of place. It was as if a bat had descended, sucked his blood perfectly clean, then flew away, without touching anything else. It was eerie. And outright terrifying. If his skin hadn't turned completely white, she would have thought he was still alive, just taking a nap. She even felt tempted to go over and feel his pulse. But she knew that would be stupid.

Sergei Rakov. He was young. And from what she'd heard, he'd been an arrogant prick. Could he already have had enemies?

What in hell could have done this? She wondered. An animal? A person? A new sort of weapon? Or had he done it to himself?

"The angle of attack rules out suicide," Detective Ramos said, standing at her side with his notepad and, as always, reading her mind.

"I want everything you have on him," she said. "I want to know who he owed money to. I want to know who his enemies were—I want to know his ex-girlfriends, his future wives. I want it all. He may have pissed the wrong people off."

"Yes, mam," he said, and hurried from the room.

Why would they pick this exact time to murder him? Why intermission? Were they sending some sort of message?

She walked slowly in the heavily carpeted room, circling, looking at him from every possible angle. He had long, black wavy hair, and was strikingly attractive, even in death. What a waste.

At that moment, a sudden noise filled the room. All the officers turned at once. They looked up, and saw that the small TV in the corner had lit up. It played footage of the night's performance. Beethoven's Ninth filled the room.

One of the detectives approached the TV to turn it off.

"Don't," she said.

The detective stopped in mid-stride.

"I want to hear it."

She stood there, staring at Sergei, as his voice filled the room. His voice that had been alive only hours before. It was eerie.

Grace circled the room once more. This time she kneeled.

"We've already been over this room, detective," the FBI agent said, impatient.

She spotted something out of the corner of her eye. She reached down, far beneath one of the slick armchairs. She craned her neck and twisted her arm, and reached all the way under.

She finally found what she was looking for. She stood, red-faced, and held up a small piece of paper.

All of the other detectives stared back.

"A ticket stub," she said, examining it with her gloved hand. "Mezzanine Right, seat 3. From tonight's concert."

She looked up and stared hard at all of her detectives, who stared blankly back.

"You think it belonged to the killer?" one of the masked.

"Well, one thing I know," she said, taking one final look at the dead, Russian opera star. "It didn't belong to him."

*

Kyle walked down the red carpeted hallways, strutting through the thick crowd. He was annoyed, as usual. He hated crowds, and he hated Carnegie Hall. He had been to a concert here once, in the 1890s, and it had not gone well. He did not release a grudge easily.

As he marched down the hall, the high collars of his black tunic covering his neck and framing his face, people made way for him. Officers, security guards, press agents – the entire crowd parted ways.

Humans are too easy to control, he thought. *The slightest bit of mindbending, and they scurry out of the way like sheep.*

A vampire of the Blacktide Coven, Kyle had seen it all in his 3,000 plus years. He had been there when they killed Christ. He had witnessed the French Revolution. He had watched smallpox spread across Europe—and had even helped it spread. There was nothing left that could surprise them.

But this night surprised him. And he did not like to be surprised.

Normally, he would just let his usual, imposing presence speak for itself, and push his way through the crowd. Despite his years, he looked young and handsome, and people usually gave way. But he had no patience for that tonight, especially given the circumstances. He had burning questions left unanswered.

What sort of rogue vampire would be so audacious as to openly kill a human? Would choose to do so in such a public way, leaving no other possibility but for the body to be found? It went against every rule of their race. Whether you were on the good or bad side of that race, it was one line you did not cross. No one wanted that sort of attention drawn to the race. It was a breach of their creed that guaranteed only one punishment: death. A long, torturous death.

Who would be so bold to attempt such a thing? To draw so much unwanted attention from the press, the politicians, the police? And worse, to do so in his coven's territory? It made his coven look bad—worse than bad. It made them look defenseless. The entire vampire race would convene and hold them to account. And if they didn't find this rogue, it could mean an outright war. War at a time when they could not afford to have one, at just the moment they were about to execute their master plan.

Kyle walked past a female police detective, and she bumped him pretty hard. To top it off, she turned and stared at him. He was surprised. No other human in this crowd had the force of will to even take notice of him. She must be stronger than the others. Either that, or he was getting sloppy.

He doubled his mind strength, directing it right at her. She finally she shook her head, turned, and kept walking. He would have to take note of her. He looked down and saw her nameplate. Detective Grace Grant. She might end up being a problem.

Kyle continued down the hall, brushing past more reporters, past the tape, and finally past a new flock of FBI agents. He made his way to the ajar door, and looked inside. The room was filled with several more FBI agents. There was also a man in an expensive suit. From his shifting, ambitious eyes, Kyle guessed he was a politician.

"The Russian Embassy is not pleased," he snapped to the FBI agent in charge. "You realize that this is not just a matter for the New York police, or just for the American government. Sergei was a star among our national vocalists. His murder must be interpreted as an offense upon our country —"

Kyle held up his palm, and using his force of will, closed the politician's mouth. He hated listening to politicians speak, and he had heard more than enough from this one. He hated Russians, too. He hated most things, actually. But tonight, his hatred rose to a new level. His impatience was getting the best of him.

No one in the room seemed to realize that Kyle closed the politician's mouth, even the politician himself. Or perhaps they were thankful. In any case, Kyle stepped to the side, and used his mind power to suggest that everyone leave the room.

"I say that we all take a coffee break for a few minutes," the FBI agent in charge suddenly said. "Clear our heads a bit."

The crowd nodded in agreement and quickly fled from the room, as if that were the most natural thing to do. As one final step, Kyle had them close the door behind themselves. He hated the sound of human voices, and especially did not want to hear them now.

Kyle breathe deeply. Finally alone, he could let his thoughts settle entirely on this human. He went up close and pulled back Sergei's collar, revealing the bite marks. Kyle reached up and placed two pale, cold fingers over them. He held them up and took note of the distance between them.

A smaller bitespan than he would have guessed. It's a she. The rogue vampire was female. And young. The teeth were not that deep.

He placed his fingers back over the bite and closed his eyes. He tried to feel the nature of the blood, the nature of the vampire that did the biting. Finally, he opened his eyes wide in shock. He withdrew his fingers quickly. He did not like what he felt. He couldn't recognize it. It was definitely a rogue vampire. Not of his clan, or of any Clan he knew. More troubling, he could not detect what breed of vampire she was at all. In his 3,000 years, this had never happened to him before.

He raised his fingers, and tasted them. Her scent overwhelmed him. Usually, that would be enough—he'd know exactly where to find her. But still, he was at a loss. Something was obscuring his vision.

He frowned. They would have no choice in this case. They would have to rely on the human police to find her. His superiors would not be pleased.

Kyle was even more annoyed than before, if possible. He stared at Sergei, and debated what to do with him. In a few hours' time he would awake, another clan-less vampire on the loose. He could kill him right now, for good, and get it over with. He would actually quite enjoy that. The vampire race hardly needed a new addition.

But that would be granting Sergei a great gift. He would not have to suffer immortality, suffer thousands of years of survival and despair. Of endless nights. No, that would be too kind. Instead, why not make Sergei suffer along with him?

He thought about it. An opera singer. Yes. His coven would quite enjoy that. This little, Russian boy could entertain them whenever they felt like it. He would bring him back. Convert him. And have yet another minion at his disposal.

Plus, Sergei could help them find her. Her scent now ran in his blood. He could lead them to her. And then they would make her suffer.

Eight

Caitlin woke to burning pain. Her skin felt on fire, and when she tried to open her eyes, a stabbing pain forced them shut. It exploded into her skull.

She kept her eyes closed, and instead used her hands to feel around. She was lying on top of something. It felt soft, yet firm. Uneven. It couldn't be a mattress. She ran her fingers along it. It felt like plastic.

Caitlin opened her eyes, more slowly this time, and peeked down at her hands. Plastic. Black plastic. And that smell. What was it? She turned her head just a little, opened her eyes a little more, and then she realized. She was sprawled out, on her back, on a pile of garbage bags. She craned her neck. She was inside a dumpster.

She sat up with a start. The pain exploded, her neck and head splitting with pain. The stench was unbearable. She looked around, eyes open now, and was horrified. How the hell had she wound up here?

She rubbed her forehead, trying to piece together the events that got her here. She drew a blank. She tried to remember last night. She used all her force of will to summon it back. Slowly, it came…

Her fight with her mother. The subway. Meeting Jonah. Carnegie Hall. The concert. Then….then….

The hunger. The craving. Yes, the craving. Leaving Jonah. Rushing out. Roaming the halls. Then… Blank. Nothing.

Where had she gone? What had she done? And how on Earth had she ended up here? Had Jonah drugged her? Did he have his way with her, then deposit her here?

She didn't think so. She couldn't imagine he was the type. In her last memory, roaming the halls, she was alone. She had left him far behind. No. It couldn't have been him.

Then what?

Caitlin kneeled slowly on the garbage, one of her feet slipping between two bags, as she sank down further into the pit. She yanked her foot out quickly and found some solid ground, plastic bottles crunching loudly.

She looked up and saw that the metal lid to the canister was open. Had she opened it last night and climbed in here? Why would she have done that? She reached up and just barely grabbed hold of the metal bar at the top. She worried she would be strong enough to pull herself up and out.

But she tried, and was amazed to find that she pulled herself out easily: one graceful motion, and she swung her legs over the side, dropped down several feet and landed on the cement. To her surprise, she landed with great agility, the shock barely hurting her at all. What was happening to her?

Just as Caitlin landed on the New York City sidewalk, a well-dressed couple had been walking past. She startled them. They turned and stared, mortified, not seeming to comprehend why a teenage girl would suddenly jump out of a huge garbage dumpster. They gave her the strangest look, then doubled their pace, hurrying to get as far away from her as possible.

Caitlin didn't blame them. She probably would have done the same. She looked down at herself, still dressed in her cocktail attire from last night, her clothing completely soiled and covered in garbage. She stank. She tried her best to wipe it off.

While she was at it, she ran her hands quickly over her body and pockets. No phone. Her mind raced, as she tried to remember if she had taken it from the apartment.

No. She had left it in her apartment, in her bedroom, on the corner of her desk. She had meant to grab it, but had been so flustered by her Mom that she'd left it behind. *Shit.* She had also left her journal. She needed them both. And she needed a shower, and a change of clothes.

Caitlin looked down at her wrist, but her watch was gone. She must have lost it somewhere during the night. She took a step out of the alley, into the busy sidewalk, and the sunlight hit her directly in the face. Pain radiated through her forehead.

She quickly stepped back into the shade. She couldn't understand what was going on. Thankfully, it was late in the afternoon. Hopefully this hangover, or whatever it was, would pass quickly.

She tried to think. Where could she go? She wanted to call Jonah. It was crazy, because she barely knew him. And after last night, whatever she'd done, she was sure he'd never want to see her again. But, still, he was the first one who came to her mind. She wanted to hear his voice, to be with him. If nothing else, she needed him to fill her in on what had happened. She desperately want to talk to him. She needed her phone.

She would go home one last time, get her phone and her journal, and get out. She prayed her Mom wouldn't be home. Maybe, just this one time, luck would be on her side.

*

Caitlin stood outside her building and looked up apprehensively. It was sunset now, and the light didn't bother her as much. In fact, as night approached, she felt stronger with each passing hour.

She bounded up the five-story walkup with lightning speed, surprising herself. She took the steps three at a time, and her legs weren't even tired. She couldn't fathom what was happening to her body. Whatever it was, she loved it.

Her good mood dimmed as she approached her apartment door. Her heart began to pound, as she wondered if her Mom would be home. How would she react?

But as she reached for the doorknob, she was surprised to see that the door was already open, slightly ajar. Her foreboding increased. Why would it be open?

Caitlin walked tentatively into the apartment, the wood creaking beneath her feet. She slowly stepped into the foyer. There, where she'd left them, were her journal and cell. She quickly grabbed them and stuffed them into her pocket. *Good*, she thought. *One less thing to worry about.*

She was about to turn and just leave. Everything inside her screamed for her to go. But there was something that gnawed at her, something that didn't feel right in the apartment. She knew she should just go, but she couldn't get herself to. She just had to know what was wrong.

Curiosity getting the best of her, she took a few tentative steps down the hall, and turned into the living room.

She immediately wished she hadn't.

As she entered she turned her head—and suddenly raised her hands to her mouth in shock. A horrible wave of nausea hit her. She turned and vomited.

It was her Mom. Lying there, slumped against the floor, eyes open. Dead. Her mother. Dead. But how?

Blood oozed from her neck, and collected in a small puddle on the floor. There was no way she could have done it to herself. She had been killed. Murdered. But how? By who? As much as she hated her Mom, she never would have wanted her to end up like this.

The blood was still fresh, and Caitlin suddenly realized that it must have just happened. The ajar door. Had someone broken in?

She suddenly wheeled, looking all around her, feeling the hair on the back of her neck stand up. Was someone else in the apartment?

As if to answer her silent question, at that very moment, three people, dressed head to toe in black, appeared from the other room. They walked nonchalantly into the living room, heading right for Caitlin. Three men. It was hard to tell how old they were—they looked ageless—maybe, late 20s. They were all well-built. Muscular. Not an ounce of fat on them. Well groomed. And very, very pale.

One of them stepped forward.

Caitlin took a step back in fear. A new sense was coming over her, a feeling of dread. She didn't understand how, but she could sense this person's energy. And it was very, very bad.

"So," the leader said, in a dark, sinister voice. "The chicken comes home to roost."

"Who are you?" Caitlin asked, backing up. She scanned the room for a weapon of some sort. Maybe a pipe, or a bat. She started thinking of exit points. The window behind her. Did it lead to a fire escape?

"Precisely the question we wanted to ask of you," the leader said. "Your human friend had no answers," he said, gesturing at her Mom's body. "Hopefully, you will."

Human? What was this person talking about?

Caitlin took several more steps back. She didn't have much room left to go. She was almost flush against the wall. She remembered now: the window behind her *did* lead to a fire escape. She remembered sitting on it, her first day in the apartment. It was rusted. And rickety. But it seemed to work.

"That was quite a feed at Carnegie Hall," he said. The three of them slowly approached her, each taking a step forward. "Very dramatic."

Caitlin scanned her memories desperately.

Feed? Try as she could, she had absolutely no idea what he was talking about.

"Why intermission?" he asked. "What was the message you were trying to send?"

She was against the wall, and had nowhere left to go. They took another step closer. She felt certain they would kill her if she did not tell them what they wanted.

She thought as hard as she could. *Message? Intermission?* She recalled roaming the halls, the carpeted hallways, going room to room. Searching. Yes, it was coming back to her. There was an open door. A dressing room. A man inside. He had looked up at her. There had been fear in his eyes. And then…

"You were in *our* territory," he said, "and you know the rules. You are going to have to answer for this."

They took another step closer.

Crash.

At just that moment, the apartment's front door shattered open, and several uniformed policeman rushed inside, guns drawn.

"Freeze, motherfucker!" a cop screamed.

The three wheeled and stared at the cops.

They then, slowly, walked towards them, completely unafraid.

"I said FREEZE!"

The leader kept walking, and the cop fired. The noise was deafening.

But, amazingly, the leader didn't even stop. He smiled even wider, simply reached out his hand, and caught the bullet in midair. Caitlin was shocked to see that he stopped it in mid-air, in his palm. He then held up his hand, slowly made a fist and crushed it. He opened his hand, and the dust slowly poured out onto the floor.

The cops, too, stared back in shock, mouths open.

The leader grinned even wider, reached out and grabbed the cop's shotgun. He yanked it from him, wound up and struck the cop across the face. The cop went flying backwards, knocking over several of his men.

Caitlin had seen enough.

Without hesitating, she turned, opened the window and climbed through. She jumped onto the fire escape and raced down the rickety, rusted steps.

She ran for all she was worth, twisting and turning. The old fire escape probably hadn't been used in years, and as she rounded a corner, a step gave way. She slipped and screamed, but then caught her balance. The entire fire escape shifted and swayed, but it didn't give completely.

She had descended three flights when she heard the noise. She looked up, and saw the three of them jump onto the fire escape. They started descending, impossibly fast. Much faster than her. She increased her pace.

She reached the first floor, and saw that there was nowhere to go: it was a 15 foot jump down to the sidewalk. She turned her neck, saw that they were coming. She looked back down. No choice. She jumped.

Caitlin braced herself for the impact, and expected it to be bad. But to her surprise, she landed she landed lithely on her feet, like a cat, with hardly any pain. She took off at a sprint, feeling confident she would leave her pursuers, whoever they were, far behind.

As she reached the end of the block, surprised by her incredible speed, she looked back, expecting to see them far away on the horizon.

But she was shocked to see that they were only a few feet behind her. How was that possible?

Before she could finish the thought, she felt bodies on top of her. They were already tackling her down to the ground.

Caitlin summoned all of her newfound strength to fight off her attackers. She elbowed one of them, and was pleasantly surprised to see him go flying several feet. Encouraged, she wheeled over and elbowed the other one, and was again happily surprised to see him go flying in the other direction.

The leader landed squarely on top of her, and began to choke her. He was stronger than the others. She looked up into his large, coal black eyes, and it was like staring into the eyes of a shark. Soulless. It was the look of death.

Caitlin used all her might, every last ounce of her strength, and managed to roll and throw him off of her. She jumped back to her feet, once again in a sprint.

But she hadn't gotten far before she felt herself tackled once again, by the leader. How could he be that fast? She had just thrown him across the alley.

This time, before she could fight back, she felt knuckles across her cheek, and realized he had just backhanded her. Hard. The world spun. She regained consciousness quickly, and prepared to fight back, when suddenly she saw the two others kneeling beside her, pinning her down. The leader extracted a cloth from his pocket.

Before she could react, the cloth was over her nose and mouth.

As she took one last, deep breath, the world spun, turned foggy.

Before the world turned to complete blackness, she could have sworn she heard a dark voice whisper in her ear: "You are ours, now."

Nine

Caitlin woke to complete blackness. She felt a cold, metal pain on her wrists and ankles, and her limbs were sore. She realized she was chained. Standing. Her arms were outstretched, by her sides, and she tried to move them, but they didn't budge. Neither did her feet. She heard a rattle as she tried, and felt the cold, hard metal dig harder into her wrists and ankles. Where the hell was she?

Caitlin opened her eyes wider, heart pounding, trying to get a feel for where she was. It was cold. She was still dressed, but barefoot, and she could feel cold stone beneath her feet. She also felt stone along her back. She was up against a wall. Chained to a wall.

She looked hard about the room and tried to make something out. But the blackness was absolute. She was cold. And thirsty. She swallowed, and her throat was dry.

She tugged for all she was worth, but even with her newfound strength, the chains did not budge. She was completely stuck.

Caitlin opened her mouth to yell for help. The first attempt didn't work. Her mouth was too dry. She swallowed again.

"Help!" she screamed, her voice coming out raspy. "HELP!" she screamed again, and this time gained real volume.

Nothing. She listened hard. She heard a faint, swooshing noise somewhere in the distance. But from where?

She tried to remember. Where was she last?

She remembered going home. Her apartment. She frowned, remembering her Mom. Dead. She felt deeply sorry, as if somehow it were her fault. And she felt remorse. She wished that she could have been a better daughter, even if her Mom wasn't great to her. Even if, as her Mom had blurted out the day before, she wasn't really even her daughter. Had she really meant it? Or was it just something she had thrown out in a time of anger?

Then...those three people. Dressed in black. So pale. Approaching her. Then... The police. The bullet. How they had stopped the bullet? What were these men? Why had they used the word "human"? She would have thought that they were merely delusional, if she had not seen them stop that bullet in mid air.

Then...the alley. The chase.

And then.... Blackness.

Caitlin suddenly heard the creak of a metal door. She squinted, as a light appeared in the distance. It was a torch. Someone was coming towards her, carrying a torch.

As he got closer, the room lit up. She was in a large, cacophonous room, entirely carved from stone. It looked ancient.

As the man got close, Caitlin could see his features. He held the torch up, to his face. He stared at her as if she were an insect.

This man was grotesque. His face was distorted, making him look like an old, haggard witch. He grinned, and revealed rows of small, orange teeth. His breath stank. He came within inches of her, and stared. He raised a hand to her face, and she could see his long, curved, yellow fingernails. Like claws. He dragged them slowly along her cheek, not enough to draw blood, but enough to make her repulsed. He grinned even wider.

"Who are you?" Caitlin asked, terrified. "Where am I?"

He only grinned further, as if examining his prey. He stared at her throat, and licked his lips.

Just then, Caitlin heard the sound of another metal door opening, and saw several torches approaching.

"Leave her!" shouted a voice from the distance. The man standing before Caitlin quickly scurried away, backing up several feet. He lowered his head, admonished.

A whole group of torches approached, and as they got close, she could see their leader. The man who had chased her down the alley.

He stared back, offering a smile with the warmth of ice. He was beautiful, this man, ageless, but terrifying. Evil. His large, charcoal eyes stared at her.

He was flanked by five other men, all dressed in black like him, but none as large or as beautiful as he. There were also two women in the group, who stared back at her with equal coldness.

"You must excuse our attendant," the man said, his voice deep, cold, and matter-of-fact.

"Who are you?" Caitlin asked. "Why am I here?"

"Forgive these harsh accommodations," the man said, running his hand along the thick metal chain that held her to the wall. "We'd be more than happy to let you go," he said, "if only you would answer a few questions."

She looked back, unsure what to say.

"I will begin. My name is Kyle. I am Deputy Leader of the Blacktide Coven," he paused. "Your turn."

"I don't know what you want from me," Caitlin answered.

"To start with, your coven. Who do you belong to?"

Caitlin wracked her brain, trying to figure out if she had lost her mind. Was she imagining all of this? She thought she must be stuck in some sort of sick dream. But she felt the very real cold steel on her wrists and ankles, and knew she was not. She had no idea what to tell this man. What was he talking about? Coven? As in…vampire?

"I don't belong to anyone," she said.

He stared for a long while, then slowly shook his head.

"As you wish. We have dealt with rogue vampires before. It's always the same: they come to test us. To see how secure our territory is. After that, more follow. That's how territory shifts begin.

"But you see, they never get away with it. Ours is the oldest strongest and coven in this land. No one kills here and gets away with it.

"So I ask again: who sent you? When do they plan to invade?"

Territory? Invasions? Caitlin couldn't understand how she was not dreaming. Maybe she had been slipped some sort of drug. Maybe Jonah had slipped her something. But she didn't drink. And she never did drugs. She was not dreaming. This was real. Too awfully, incredibly real.

She could've just dismissed them as a group of completely crazy people, as some weird cult or society that was completely delusional. But after all that had happened in the last 48 hours, she actually found herself thinking twice. Her own strength. Her own behavior. The way she felt her body changing. Could vampires be true? Was she one of them? Had she stumbled into the middle of some kind of vampire war? That would be just her luck.

Caitlin stared back, thinking. Had she really killed someone? Who? She couldn't remember, but she had this awful feeling that what he said was true. That she *had* killed someone. That, more than anything, made her feel terrible. She felt an awful feeling of pity and regret wash over her. If it was true, she was a murderer. She could never live that down.

She stared back at him.

"I wasn't sent by anyone," she said, finally. "I don't remember exactly what I did. But whatever I did, I did it on my own. I don't really know why I did it. I'm really sorry for whatever I did," she said. "I didn't mean it."

Kyle turned and looked at the others. They looked back at him. He shook his head, and turned back to her. His glare turned cold and hard.

"You take me for a fool, I see. Not wise."

Kyle gestured to his subordinates, and they hurried over and uncuffed her chains. She felt her arms drop, and was relieved to have the blood flow back to her wrists. They uncuffed her ankles next. Four of them, two on one each side, got a tight grip on her arms and shoulders.

"If you won't answer to me," Kyle said, "then you will answer to the Assembly. Just remember, you have chosen this. They will show no mercy, as I may have done."

As they led her away, Kyle added, "Make no mistake, you will be killed either way. But my way would have been quick and painless. Now you will see what suffering is."

Caitlin tried to resist as they dragged her forward. But it was useless. They were leading her somewhere, and there was nothing she could do but embrace her fate.

And pray.

*

When they opened the oak door, Caitlin could not believe her eyes. The room was enormous. Shaped in a huge circle, it was lined with hundred-foot-tall stone columns, ornately decorated. It was well lit, torches placed every 5 feet, all throughout the room. It looked like the Pantheon. It looked ancient.

As she was led in, the next thing she noticed was the noise. It was a huge crowd. She looked around and saw hundreds, if not thousands, of men and women dressed in black, moving quickly all about the room. There was a strangeness to how they moved: it was so fast, so random, so…inhuman.

She heard a swooshing noise, and looked up. Dozens of these people leapt, or flew, through the room, going from floor to ceiling, from ceiling to balcony, from column to ledge. That was the whooshing noise she had heard. It was as if she had entered a cave full of bats.

She took it all in and was completely, utterly, shocked. Vampires did exist. Was she one of them?

They led her to the center of the room, chains rattling, her bare feet cold on the stone. They led her to a spot in the center of the floor, designated by a large, tile circle.

As she reached the center, the noise gradually died down. The motion slowed. Hundreds of vampires took positions in a huge, stone amphitheater before her. It looked like a political assembly, like the pictures she had seen of the state of the union address—except, instead of hundreds of politicians, these were hundreds of vampires, all staring at her. Their order and discipline was impressive. Within seconds, they were all perfectly seated, quiet as can be. The room fell silent.

As she stood in the center of the room, held in place by the attendants, Kyle stepped off to the side, folded his hands, and lowered his head in reverence.

Before the assembly sat an immense stone chair. It looked like a throne. She looked up and saw that seated in it was a vampire who looked older than the others. She could tell that he was absolutely ancient. There was something about his cold, blue eyes. They stared down at her as if they had seen 10,000 years. She hated the feeling of his eyes on her. They were evil itself.

"So," he said, his voice a low rumble. "This is the one who breached our territory," he said. His voice was gravelly and had absolutely no warmth in it. It echoed in the huge chamber.

"Who is your coven leader?" he asked.

Caitlin stared back, debating how to answer. She had no idea what to say.

"I don't have a leader," she said. "And I don't belong to any coven. I am here by myself."

"You know the punishment for trespass," he stated, a smile growing at the corner of his mouth. "If there is anything worse than immortality," he continued, "it is immortality in pain."

He stared at her.

"This is your last chance," he said.

She stared back, having no idea what to say. Out of the corner of her eye, she scanned the room for an exit, wondering if there was any way out. She didn't see one.

"As you wish," he said, and nodded ever so slightly.

A side door opened, and out came a vampire in chains, dragged by two attendants. He was dragged to the center of the floor, only feet from where Caitlin stood. She watched in fear, unsure what was happening.

"This vampire broke the rule of mating," the leader said. "Not as severe a violation as yours. But still, one that must be punished."

The leader nodded again, and an attendant stepped forward with a small vial of liquid. He reached up and splashed it on the chained vampire.

The chained vampire started shrieking. Caitlin watched his skin bubble up all over his arm, welts appearing immediately, as if he were burned. His shrieks were horrific.

"This is not just any holy water," the leader said, staring down at Caitlin, "but specially charged water. From the Vatican. I assure you that it will burn through any skin, and that the pain will be horrific. Worse than acid."

He stared long and hard Caitlin. The room was completely silent.

"Tell us where you're from and you will be spared an awful death."

Caitlin swallowed hard, not wanting to feel that water on her skin. It looked horrific. Then again, if she were not truly a vampire, it shouldn't harm her. But it was not an experiment she wanted to take.

She pulled again at her chains, but they did not give way.

73

She could feel her heart pounding, and the sweat raising on her brow. What could she possibly tell him?

He stared at her, judging her up.

"You are brave. I admire your loyalty to your coven. But your time is up."

He nodded, and she heard the sound of chains. She looked over, and saw two attendants hoist a huge cauldron. With each pull, they raised it several feet in the air. When it was high, about 15 feet off the ground, they swung it over, so that it was directly over her head.

"There were but a few ounces of holy water splashed on that vampire," the leader said. "Above you sit *gallons*. When it washes over your body, it will give you the most horrific pain imaginable. You will be in this pain for a lifetime. But you will still be alive, immobile, helpless. Remember, you have chosen this."

The man nodded, and Caitlin felt her heart pounding ten times the speed. The attendants at her side hooked her chains into the stone and ran, rushing to get as far away from her as possible.

As Caitlin looked up, she saw the cauldron tilting, and the liquid begin to pour. She looked back down and closed her eyes.

Please God. Help me!

"No!" she screamed, her scream echoing through the chamber.

And then, she was immersed.

Ten

The water covered her entire body, making it hard to breathe, or open her eyes. After about ten seconds, though, after her entire hair and body and clothes were completely drenched, Caitlin blinked her eyes. She braced herself for the pain.

But it didn't come.

She blinked, then looked up at the cauldron, wondering if it were completely empty. It was. She looked back down at herself, and saw she was drenched. But she was completely fine. Not an ounce of pain.

The leader, suddenly realizing, stood in his chair, jaw dropping. He was clearly shocked. Kyle, too, turned and looked, his mouth open. The entire assembly, hundreds of vampires, all stood, and a gasp spread through the room.

Caitlin could see that this was not the reaction they had been expecting. They were all dumbfounded.

Somehow, their water had not affected her. Maybe she wasn't a vampire after all?

Caitlin saw her chance.

While they all stood there, too shocked to react, she summoned her strength and in one motion, broke her chains. She then took off at a sprint away from the assembly, in the direction of that side door. She prayed it led somewhere.

She made it halfway across the room before anyone could get over their shock to react.

"Get her!" she finally heard the leader scream.

And then, the sound of hundreds of bodies rustling towards her. The noise bounced off the walls, came from everywhere, and she realized that they were not just running towards her, but jumping down off the ceilings, off the balconies, their wings spread, speeding towards her. They swept down towards her, like a vulture after its prey, and she doubled her speed, ran for everything she had.

She fumbled in the dark, led only by the torches, and as she rounded a bend, finally, in the distance, she saw the door. It was open. And light came from behind it. It was indeed an exit, and it would have been perfect. Except for that one, last vampire.

Standing before the door, blocking her path, was a large, well sculpted vampire, completely draped in black. He looked younger than the others, maybe 20, and his features were more chiseled. Even in her haste, even with her life in such danger, Caitlin could not help but noticing how strikingly attractive this vampire was. Still, he was blocking her only way out.

She could outrun the others, but she could not get past this man without going right through him. He opened the door even wider, as if making way for her to pass through it. Was he tricking her? She looked down and saw that he held a long spear in his hand.

As she got closer, he held it up and aimed it right for her. She was only feet from the door now, and she couldn't stop. They were on her tail, and if she even slowed, it would be the end of her. So she ran right for him, closing her eyes and bracing herself for the inevitable impact of his spear running through her body. At least it would be quick.

As she opened her eyes she saw him releasing his spear, and she reflexively ducked.

But he had aimed too high. Way too high. She craned her neck back, and saw that he had not been aiming at her after all, but at one of the vampires who had been swooping down at her. The silver-tipped spear pierced the vampire's throat, and a hideous screech filled the room, as the creature fell to the ground.

Caitlin stared at this new vampire in wonder. He had just saved her. Why?

"Go!" he screamed.

She picked up her pace and ran right through the open door.

As she turned around, he turned with her and yanked closed the door with all his might, closing it firmly behind them. He quickly reached up, foisted an enormous metal shaft, and placed it across the door, barring it. He took several steps back, standing next to her, watching the door.

She couldn't help looking up at him, studying the line of his jaw, his brown hair and brown eyes. He had saved her. Why?

But he wasn't looking back down at her. He was still watching the door, fear in his eyes. With good reason. Within a second of his having barred it, a body had hurled against it. The door was over six feet thick, pure steel, and the bars were even thicker. But it was no match. The bodies crashed into it from the other side, and the door was already almost completely caved in. It would only be seconds until they crashed through.

"Move!" he shouted, and before she could react, he grabbed her arm and led her away. He tugged at her, making her run faster than she ever had, faster than she knew she could, and within seconds they were down one hall, then another, then another, twisting and turning every which way. The only thing they had to see by were occasional torches. She never could have made it out of there on her own.

"What's going on?" Caitlin tried to ask as they ran, out of breath. "Where are we —"

"This way!" he yelled, yanking her suddenly in another direction.

Behind them, Caitlin heard a crashing, followed by the sound of a mob, bearing down on them.

They reached a circular staircase, made of stone, winding its way up along a wall. He ran full speed toward the steps, yanking her with him, and before she knew it they were racing up the steps, twisting in circles, taking them three at a time. They were ascending quickly.

As they reached the top, it seemed to end in a complete wall. A stone ceiling was above them, and she could see no other way out. It was a dead-end. Where had he led them?

He was confused, too. And angry. But he seemed determined. He took a few steps back, and with a running start, charged at the ceiling. It was incredible. With this superhuman strength, he smashed a hole right through. Stone crumbled, and light poured through. Real, electric light. Where were they?

"Come on!" he yelled.

He reached down and grabbed her arm, yanking her up and out, through the ceiling, and into the well-lit room.

She looked about. It looked like they were in a courthouse. Or a museum. It was a grand, beautiful structure. The floors were marble, the room was all stone, columns. It was round. It looked like a government building.

"Where are we?" she asked.

He grabbed her hand and took off at a sprint, tugging her through the room at lightning speed. He charged a set of two huge, steel doors. He let go of her wrist and ran right into them, leaning his shoulder hard. They flew open with a crash.

She followed close behind, this time not waiting. She heard the sound of stone moving behind her, and knew that the mob was close.

They were outside, finally, and the cold, night air struck her in the face. She was so grateful to be out from underground.

She tried to get her bearings. They were definitely in New York. But where? Her surroundings seemed vaguely familiar. She saw a city street, a passing taxi. She turned to look back, and saw the structure they had just left. City Hall. The coven had been beneath City Hall.

They ran down the steps and across the courtyard, heading for the street. They hadn't gotten far when there came the noise of doors opening behind him, and a mob of vampires.

They headed right for a large, iron gate. As they got close, two security officers. They turned around, and saw them running right for the gate. Their eyes opened wide in shock, and they reached for their guns.

"Don't move!" they yelled.

Before they could react, he grabbed her tight, took three long bounds, and leapt for all he was worth. She felt them flying through the air, 10 feet, 20, clearing the metal gate and landing on the other side with grace.

They hit the ground running. She looked at her protector in shock, wondering what the extent of his power was. Wondering why he cared about her. And wondering, why she felt so good beside him.

Before she could think much longer, there was the crash of metal behind them, followed by gunshots. The other vampires had broken through, taking the police officers down with them. They were already close behind.

They ran and ran but it was not working. The mob was fast closing in.

He suddenly grabbed her hand and turned the corner, taking them down a side street. It ended in a wall.

"It's a dead-end!" she yelled. But he kept running, dragging her with him.

He reached the end of the alley, dropped to a knee, and with a single finger reached in and yanked up a huge, iron manhole.

She turned, and saw the huge group of vampires heading right towards them, not more than 20 feet away

"Go!" he yelled, and before she could react, he grabbed her and shoved her into the hole.

She grabbed hold of the ladder, and as she looked up, she saw him get on his hands and knees, bracing himself. He raised the manhole cover as a shield.

He was descended upon by the mob. He swung wildly, and she heard the impact as he knocked vampire after vampire away with the heavy iron. He was trying to join her, to get into the hole, too, but he couldn't make it. He was surrounded.

She was about to climb up and help him, when suddenly, one of the vampires parted from the mob and slipped into the hole. He spotted Caitlin, hissed, and came right for her.

She scrambled down the ladder, taking them two rings of the time, but it wasn't fast enough. He landed on top of her, and they both started falling.

As she fell through the air, she braced herself for the impact. Luckily, they landed in water.

As she rose, she saw she was in up to her waist in filthy, sewage water.

She had barely time to think when the vampire landed beside her with a splash. With one motion, he wound back and backhanded her across the face, sending her flying several feet.

She landed on her back in the water, and looked up to see him pouncing again, right for her throat. She rolled out of the way just in time, springing back on her feet. He was fast, but so was she.

He fell flat on his face. He got up and spun around and squared off in a rage. He clawed his right hand right for her face. She dodged it, and his hand barely missed her, the wind of it passing right by her cheek. His hand hit the wall with such force that it lodged into the stone.

Caitlin was mad now. She felt the red-hot rage pulse in her veins. She walked over to the stuck vampire and wound back her leg and planted a strong kick right in his gut. He keeled over.

She then grabbed him from behind and threw him right into the wall, face first. His head hit the stone hard. She was proud of herself, figuring she had finished him off.

But she was shocked by a sudden pain in her face, and found herself backhanded once again. This vampire had recovered quickly—much more quickly than she had thought possible. Before she knew it, he was on top of her. He landed on her with a crash and brought her down. She had underestimated him.

His hand was on her throat, and on it for real. She was strong, but he was stronger. He had an ancient strength that ran through his body. His hand was cold and clammy. She tried to resist, but it was just too much. She dropped to one knee, and he kept squeezing. Before she knew it, he was pushing her head towards the water. At the last second, she managed a scream: "Help!"

A second later, her head was submerged.

*

Caitlin felt the disruption in the water, the waves rushing, and knew that someone else had landed in the water. She was losing oxygen fast, unable to fight back.

Caitlin felt strong arms under her, and felt herself being hoisted up and out of the water.

She jumped up and gasped for breath, sucking it in deeper than she ever had. She breathed again and again, hyperventilating.

"Are you okay?" he asked, holding her shoulders.

She nodded. That was all she could manage. She looked over and saw that her attacker lay there, floating in the water, on his back. Blood was oozing out of his neck. He was dead.

She looked up at him, his brown eyes looking down at her. He had saved her. Again.

"We've got to move," he said, grabbing her arm and leading her, sloshing, through the waist-high water. "That manhole won't hold very long."

As if on cue, the manhole above them was suddenly torn out.

They ran. They turned down tunnel after tunnel, and heard the sound of water sloshing behind them.

He made a sharp turn and the water level dropped down to their ankles. They picked up real speed.

They entered yet another tunnel, and found themselves in the midst of major New York City infrastructure. There were massive steam pipes here, letting off huge clouds of steam. The heat was unbearable.

He took her down yet another tunnel, and suddenly picked her up and placed her on his back, wrapping her arms around his chest, and ascended a ladder, taking three rungs at a time. They were rising, and as he reached the top, he punched a manhole and sent it flying out before them.

They were back above ground, on New York City streets. Where, she had no idea.

"Hold on tight," he said, and she tightened her grip around his chest, clasping her hands into each other. He ran, and ran, and it turned into a sprint, at a speed beyond which she had never experienced. She had a memory of riding on the back of a motorcycle once, years ago, and the feeling of the wind whipping through her hair at 60 miles an hour. It felt like that. But faster.

They must have been doing 80 miles an hour, then 100, then 120… It just kept going. The buildings, people, cars—it all became a blur. And before she knew it, they were off the ground.

They were in the air, flying. He opened his huge, black wings, flapping slowly beside her. They were up above the cars, above the people. She looked down and saw that they flew over 14th Street. Then, a few seconds later, 34th. A few more seconds, and they were above Central Park. It took her breath away.

He checked back over their shoulders, and so did she. She could barely see, with the wind whipping in her eyes, but she could see enough to know that no one, no creature, was following them.

He slowed a bit, and then dipped, lowering their height. Now they flew just above the tree line. It was beautiful. She had never seen Central Park this way, its pathways lit up, the treetops right below her. She felt like she could reach out and touch them. She had a feeling that it would never look as beautiful as it did right now.

She clasped her hands tighter around his chest, feeling his warmth. She felt safe. As surreal as all of this was, things felt back to normal in his arms. She wanted to fly like this forever. As she closed her eyes and felt the cool breeze caress her face, she prayed that this night would never end.

Eleven

Caitlin felt them slow, and then begin to descend. She opened her eyes. She didn't recognize any of the buildings below them. It appeared that they were way uptown. Possibly, the Bronx somewhere.

As they descended, they flew over a small park, and in the distance, she thought she saw a castle. As they got closer, she realized that it definitely was a castle. What was a castle doing here, in New York City?

She wracked her brain, and realized that she had seen this castle before. On a postcard somewhere...Yes. It was a museum of some sort. As they ascended a small hill, flying over its ramparts, flying over its small, medieval walls, she suddenly remembered what it was. The Cloisters. The small museum. It had been brought over from Europe, piece by piece. It was hundreds of years old. Why was he taking her here?

They descended smoothly over the outer wall and onto a large, stone terrace, overlooking the Hudson river. They landed in darkness, but his feet touched down gracefully on the stone, and he gently let her off.

She stood there, facing him. She looked at him closely, hoping that he was still real, hoping that he wouldn't fly away. And hoping that he was as gorgeous as he was the first time she saw him.

He was. If anything, even more so. He stared down at her with his large, brown eyes, and at that moment she felt herself get lost.

There are so many questions she wanted to ask, she didn't even know where to begin. Who was he? How was he able to fly? Was he a vampire? Why had he risked his life for her? Why take her here? And most importantly, was everything she had seen just a wild hallucination? Or did vampires really exist, right here in New York City? And was she one of them?

She opened her mouth to speak, but all she managed was: "Why are we here?"

She knew it was a stupid question the moment she asked it, and hated herself for not asking something more important. But standing there in the cold, March night, face a bit numb, it was the best she could do.

He just stared back at her. His stare seemed to pierce her soul, as if he were seeing right through her. It looked as if he were debating how much to tell her.

Finally, after what seemed an eternity, he opened his mouth to speak.

"Caleb!" shouted a voice, and they both turned.

A group of men – vampires? – dressed all in black, marched right for them. Caleb turned and faced them. *Caleb. She liked that.*

"We have no clearance for your arrival," the man in the middle said, deadly serious.

"It is unannounced," Caleb answered flatly.

"Then we will have to take you into custody," he said, nodding to his men, who slowly circled behind Caleb and her. "The rules."

Caleb nodded, unfazed. The man in the middle looked directly at Caitlin. She could see the disapproval in his eyes.

"You know we can't let her in," the man said to Caleb.

"But you will," Caleb answered flatly. He stared back at the man, equally determined. It was a meeting of the wills.

The man stood there, and she could see he was unsure what to do. A long, tense silence followed.

"Very well," he said, turning his back abruptly and leading the way. "It's your funeral."

Caleb followed, and Caitlin walked beside him, unsure what else to do.

The man opened a huge, medieval door, grabbing it by its round, brass ring. He then stepped aside, motioning for Caleb to enter. Two more men, in black, stood inside the doorway, standing at attention.

Caleb took Caitlin's hand and led her through. As she passed through the huge stone archway, she felt as if she were entering another century.

"Guess we don't have to pay admission," Caitlin said to Caleb, smiling.

He looked over at her, blinking. It took him a second to realize it was a joke. Finally, he smiled.

He had a beautiful smile.

It made her think of Jonah. She felt confused. It was unlike her to feel strong feelings for any boy—much less for two of them in the same day. She still felt for Jonah. But Caleb was different. Jonah was a boy. Caleb, although he looked young, was a man. Or was he…something else? There was something about him she could not explain, something that made her unable to look away. Something that made her not want to leave his side. She liked Jonah. But she *needed* Caleb. Being around him was all-encompassing.

Caleb's smile vanished as quickly as it had appeared. He was clearly disturbed.

"I'm afraid there will be a much higher price for admission," he said, "if this meeting does not go as I would hope."

He led her through another stone archway, and into a small, medieval courtyard. Perfectly symmetrical, surrounded on four sides by columns and arches, this courtyard, lit by the moon, was very beautiful. She could not fathom how they were still in New York City. They could have been in a European countryside.

They walked across the courtyard and down a long stone hallway, the sound of their footsteps echoing. They were trailed by several more guards. Vampires? She wondered. If so, why were they so civil? Why didn't they attack Caleb, or her?

They walked down another stone corridor and through another medieval door. And then they suddenly stopped.

Standing there was another man, dressed in black, who looked startlingly similar to Caleb. He wore a large red cloak over his shoulders, and was flanked by several attendants. He seemed to hold a position of authority.

"Caleb," he said softly. He sounded shocked to see him.

Caleb stood there calmly, staring back.

"Samuel," Caleb answered, flatly.

The man stood there, staring, shaking his head just a little bit.

"Not even a hug for your long lost brother?" Caleb asked.

"You know this is very serious," Samuel answered. "You have violated many laws by coming here tonight. Especially by bringing her."

The man did not even bother looking over at Caitlin. She felt insulted.

"But I had no choice," Caleb said. "The day has arrived. War is here."

A hushed murmur erupted among the vampires standing behind Samuel, and among the growing group of vampires forming behind them. She turned, and saw that more than a dozen of them now encircled them. She was starting to feel claustrophobic. They were vastly outnumbered, and there was no way out. She had no idea what Caleb had done, but whatever it was, she hoped that he could talk his way out of it.

Samuel raised his hands, and the murmur died down.

"What's more," Caleb continued, "this woman here," he said, nodding towards Caitlin, "she is The One."

Woman. Caitlin had never been called that before. She liked it. But she didn't understand. *The One?* He had put a funny emphasis on the phrase, as if he were talking about the Messiah or something. She wondered if they were all crazy.

Another murmur arose, and all heads turned to stare at her.

"I need to see the Council," Caleb said, "And I must bring her with me."

Samuel shook his head.

"You know that I would not stop you. I can only advise. And I advise you to leave right now, return to your post and await the Council's summons."

Caleb stared back. "I'm afraid that is not possible," he said.

"You've always done as you wish," Samuel said.

Samuel stepped aside, and motioned with his hand that he was free to pass.

"Your wife will not be pleased," Samuel said.

Wife? Caitlin thought, and felt a cold chill run up her spine. Why did she suddenly feel so insanely jealous? How had her feelings for Caleb developed that quickly? What right did she have to feel so possessive of him?

She felt her cheeks turn red. She *did* care. It made no sense at all, but she completely cared. *Why didn't he tell me–*

"Don't call her that," Caleb answered, his cheeks also burning red. "You know that –"

"Know that *what*?" came a woman's shriek.

They all turned to see a woman marching towards them from down the hallway. She, too, was dressed in all black, with long, flowing red hair that trailed past her shoulders, and large, shiny green eyes. She was tall, ageless, and strikingly beautiful.

Caitlin felt humbled in her presence, like she had just shrunk. *This* was a woman. Or was it…vampire? Whatever she was, she was a creature that Caitlin could never compete with. She felt deflated, prepared to concede Caleb to whoever she was.

"Know that *what*?" the woman repeated, staring harshly at Caleb as she walked up to him, just a few feet away. She glanced over at Caitlin, and her mouth curled into a snarl. Caitlin had never seen anyone look at her with so much hatred before.

"Sera," Caleb said softly, "we have not been married for 700 years."

"In your eyes, maybe," she snapped back.

She started to pace, circling both Caitlin and Caleb. She looked her up and down as if she were an insect.

"How dare you bring *her* here," she spat. "Really. You know far better."

"She is The *One*," Caleb said flatly.

Unlike the others, this woman did not seem surprised. Instead, she just let out a short, mocking laugh.

"That's ridiculous," she answered. "You've brought war on us," she continued, "and all for a human. A simple infatuation," she said, her anger rising. With each sentence, the crowd behind her seemed to get bolstered, to grow with a concurring anger. It was becoming an angry mob.

"In fact," Sera continued, "we have the right to tear her apart."

The crowd behind her began to murmur in approval.

Anger flashed across Caleb's face.

"Then you would have to go through me," Caleb answered, staring back with equal determination.

Caitlin felt a warmth run through her. He was laying his life on the line for her. Again. Maybe he *did* care for her.

Samuel stepped forward, between them, and held out his hands. The crowd quieted.

"Caleb has requested an audience with the Council," he said. "We owe him at least that. Let him state his case. Let the Council decide."

"Why should we?" Sera snapped.

"Because that is what I said," Samuel answered, a steely determination in his voice. "And I give orders up here, Sera, not you." Samuel stared long and hard at her. Finally, she deferred.

Samuel stepped aside, and gestured towards the stone staircase.

Caleb reached out and took Caitlin's hand, and led her forward. They stepped down the wide stone steps, and descended into the darkness.

Behind her, Caitlin heard a sharp laughter cut through the night.

"Good riddance."

Twelve

Their footsteps echoed on the wide, stone staircase as they descended. It was dimly lit. Caitlin reached over and slipped her hand into Caleb's arm. She hoped that he would let it sit there. He did. In fact, he tightened his arm around hers. Once again, everything felt OK. She felt that she could descend into the depths of darkness, as long as they were together.

So many thoughts raced through her mind. What was this Council? Why had he insisted on taking her? And why did she feel so insistent on being at his side? She could have easily objected up there, told him that he did that she didn't want to go, that she'd rather wait upstairs. But she didn't want to wait upstairs. She wanted to be with him. She couldn't imagine herself anywhere else.

None of it made any sense. At every turn, instead of getting answers, all she got were new questions. Who were all those people upstairs? Were they really vampires? What were they doing here? In the Cloisters?

They turned the corner, into a large room, and she was struck by its beauty. It was incredible, like descending into a real medieval castle. Soaring ceilings capped rooms carved out of medieval stone. Off to her right there lay several sarcophagi, raised above the floor. Intricate, medieval figures were carved on their lids. Some of them were open. Was that where they slept?

She tried to think back to all the vampire lore she had ever heard. Sleeping in coffins. Awake at night. Superhuman strength and speed. Pain in the sunlight. It all seemed to add up. She herself felt some pain in the sun. But it wasn't unbearable. And she was impervious to the holy water. What's more, this place, the Cloisters, was filled with crosses: there were enormous crosses everywhere. Yet it didn't seem to affect these vampires. In fact, this seemed to be their home.

She wanted to ask Caleb about all of this, and more, but didn't know how to begin. She settled on the last one.

"The crosses," she said, nodding as they walked under another one. "Don't they bother you?"

He looked at her, not understanding. He looked like he'd been lost in thought.

"Don't crosses hurt vampires?" she asked.

Recognition crossed his face.

"Not all of us," he answered. "Our race is very fragmented. Much like the human race. There are many races within our race, and many territories—or covens—within each race. It is quite complex. They don't affect the benevolent vampires."

"Benevolent?" she asked.

"Just like your human race, there are forces for good and forces of evil. We are not all the same."

He left it at that. As usual, the answers only raised more questions. But she held her tongue. She didn't want to pry. Not now.

Despite the high ceilings, the doorways were small. The arched, wooden doors were open, and they walked right through, ducking as they went. As they enter the new room, the height opened up again, and it was another magnificent room. She looked up and could see stained glass everywhere. To her right was some sort of pulpit, and before it, dozens of tiny, wooden chairs. It was stark, and beautiful. It truly looked like some sort of medieval cloister.

She saw no sign of life, and heard no movement. She heard absolutely nothing. She wondered where they all were.

They entered another room, the floor sloping gently downward, and she gasped. This small room was filled with treasures. It was a working museum, and they were all encased carefully behind glass. Right there before her, under sharp, halogen lights, were what must have been hundreds of millions of dollars' worth of ancient, priceless treasures. Gold crosses. Large, silver goblets. Medieval manuscripts....

She followed Caleb as he walked through the room and stopped before a long, vertical, glass case. Inside was a magnificent ivory staff, several feet long. He stared at it through the glass.

He was quiet for several seconds.

"What is it?" she finally asked.

He kept staring, quietly. Finally, he said, "An old friend."

That was it. He didn't offer any more. She wondered what sort of history he had with the object, and what sort of power it held. She read the plaque: early 1300s.

"It is known as a crozier. A bishop's staff. It is both a rod and a staff. A rod for punishment and a staff for leading the faithful. The symbol of our church. It has the power to bless, or to curse. It is what we guard. It is what keeps us safe."

Their church? What they guard?

Before she could ask more questions, he took her hand and led her through yet another doorway.

They reached a velvet rope. He reached out, unclasped it, and pulled it back for her to enter. He then followed right behind her, re-clasped it, and led her to a small, circular wooden staircase. It led down, seemingly right into the floor itself. She looked at it, puzzled.

Caleb knelt and undid a secret latch in the floor. A floor trap opened up, and she could see that the staircase continued downward, into the depths.

Caleb looked right into her eyes, "Are you ready?"

She wanted to say *No*. But instead, she took his hand.

*

This staircase was narrow and steep, and led into real blackness. After winding and winding, deeper and deeper, she finally saw a light in the distance, and started to hear movement. As they turned the corner, they entered another room.

This room was huge and brightly lit, torches everywhere. It mirrored the upstairs rooms identically, with soaring, stone, medieval ceilings, arched, covered in intricate detail. There were large tapestries on the walls, and the huge space was filled with medieval furniture.

It was also filled with people. Vampires. They were all dressed in black, and they moved casually about the room. Many of them sat in various seats, some talking to each other. In the other coven, under City Hall, she had felt evil, darkness, had felt in constant danger. Here, she felt strangely relaxed.

Caleb led her across the long room, right down the center. As they walked, the movement subsided, and a hush descended. She could feel all the eyes on them.

As they reach the end of the room, Caleb approached a large vampire, taller than he was, and with much broader shoulders. The man looked down, expressionless.

"I need an audience," Caleb said simply.

The vampire slowly turned and walked through the doorway, closing the door firmly behind him.

Caleb and Caitlin stood there, waiting. She turned, and surveyed the room. They were all – hundreds of vampires – staring at them. But no one moved to come close.

The door opened, and the large vampire gestured. They entered.

This small room was darker, dimly lit by only two torches at the far end of the room. It was also completely empty, save for a long table on the opposite side. Behind it sat seven vampires, all staring grimly back. It looked like a panel of judges.

There was something about these vampires which made them look much older. There was a harshness to their expressions. Definitely a panel of judges.

"Council in session!" the large vampire yelled, banging his staff on the floor, then quickly exiting the room. He closed the door firmly behind them. It was now just the two of them, facing the seven vampires.

She stood tentatively at Caleb's side, unsure what to do, or say.

An awkward silence followed, as the judges studied them. It felt as if they were staring through their souls.

"Caleb," came a gravelly voice, from the vampire in the center of the panel. "You have abandoned your post."

"I did not, sire," he answered. "I have kept my post faithfully for 200 years. I was forced to take action tonight."

"You take no action but for our command," he answered. "You have jeopardized us all."

"My duty was to alert us for the coming war," Caleb answered. "I believe that time has come."

A gasp came from the Council. There was a long silence.

"And what makes you think this?"

"They doused her in holy water, and it did not burn her skin. Doctrine tells us that the day will come when the One will arrive, and will be impervious to our weapons. And that she will herald war."

A hushed gasp spread across the room. They all stared at Caitlin, scrutinizing her. Several of the judges began talking amongst themselves, until finally the one in the middle slammed the table with his palm.

"Silence!" He yelled.

Gradually, the murmur died down.

"So, You risked us all to save a human?" he asked.

"I saved her to save ourselves," Caleb answered. "If she is the One, we are nothing without her."

Caitlin's head spun, She didn't know what to think. *The One? Doctrine? What was he talking about?* She wondered if he thought she was someone else, thought she was someone greater than she is.

Her heart sank, not because of the way that the Council looked at her, but because she began to worry that Caleb had only saved her for his own sake. That he didn't really care for her. And that his affection for her would disappear when he knew the truth. He would find out that she was just an average, ordinary girl, no matter what took place over the last few days, and he would abandon her. Just like all the other guys in her life.

As if to confirm her thoughts, the judge in the middle slowly shook his head, staring at Caleb with condescension.

"You have made a grave mistake," he said. "What you fail to see is that *you* are the one who began this war. Your departure is what has alerted them to our presence.

"Furthermore, she is not the one you think she is."

Caleb began, "Then how do you explain–"

Another council member spoke this time, "Many centuries ago there was a case like this. A vampire was immune to weaponry. People thought he was the Messiah then, too. He was not. He was just a half-breed."

"Half-breed?" Caleb asked. He suddenly sounded unsure.

"The vampire by birth," he continued, "one that was never turned. They are immune to some weaponry, but not to others. But that does not make them one of us. Nor does it make them immortal. I'll show you," he continued, and suddenly turned to Caitlin.

She felt nervous with his eyes staring through her. "Tell me young one, who turned you?"

Caitlin had no idea what he was talking about. She didn't even know what his question meant. Once again this night, she found herself wondering what the best answer was to give. She hesitated, feeling that whatever she said would have a great impact not just on her safety, but on Caleb's, too. She wanted to give the right answer for him, but she just didn't know what to say.

"I'm sorry," she said, "I don't know what you're talking about. I was never turned. I don't even know what that means."

Another council member leaned forward. "Then who is your father?" he asked.

Of all questions, why had he had to ask her that? That was the question she had always asked herself, her whole life long. Who was he? Why had she never met him? Why did he leave her? It was an answer she wanted more than anything in life. And now, on demand, she certainly could not provide it.

"I don't know," she said, finally.

The council member leaned back, as if in victory. "You see?" he said. "Half-breeds are not turned. And they never know their parents. You are mistaken, Caleb. You have made a grave error."

"Doctrine states that a half-breed will be the Messiah, and that she will lead us to the lost sword," Caleb snapped back, defiantly.

"Doctrine states that a half-breed will *bring* the Messiah," the council member corrected. "Not *be*."

"You are parsing words," Caleb answered. "I am telling you that war has begun, and that she will lead us to the sword. Time is swift. We must have her lead us to it. It is the only hope we have."

"A child's tales," answered another council member. "The sword you speak of does not exist. And if it did, a half-breed would not be the one to lead us."

"If we don't, others will. They will capture her, and find it, and use it against us."

"You have committed a grave violation in bringing her here," another one of them said, from the far end of the panel.

"But I—" Caleb began.

"ENOUGH!" shouted the lead council member.

The room grew silent.

"Caleb. You have knowingly violated several laws of our coven. You have abandoned your post. You have disgraced your mission.

You have sparked a war. And you have risked us all for a human. Not even a human, but a half-breed. Worse, you have brought her here, right into our midst, endangering us all.

"We sentence you to 50 years confinement. You will not leave these grounds. And you will cast this half-breed out of our walls at once.

"Now, leave us."

Thirteen

Caitlin and Caleb stood together on the large, open terrace outside the Cloisters, looking out at the night. Far-off, she could see the Hudson River, peeking out between the bare trees of March. In the distance, she could even see the tiny lights of cars heading over the bridge. The night was completely silent.

"I need you to answer some questions for me, Caleb," she said softly, after several seconds of silence.

"I know," Caleb answered.

"What am I doing here? Who do you think I am?" Caitlin asked. It took her a few seconds more to summon the courage to ask the final question, "And why did you save me?"

Caleb stared off into the horizon for several seconds. She could not tell what he was thinking, or if he would even answer.

Finally, he turned to her. He stared right into her eyes, and the power of his stare was overwhelming. She couldn't look away if she tried.

"I am a vampire," he said, flatly. "Of the White Coven. I have lived for over 3,000 years, and I have been with this coven for 800 of them."

"Why am I here?"

"Vampire covens and races are always at war. They are very territorial. Unfortunately, you stumbled right into the middle of it."

"What do you mean?" she asked. "How?"

He looked at her, confused. "Don't you remember?"

She stared back, blankly.

"Your kill. It ignited all of this."

"Kill?"

He slowly shook his head. "So, you don't remember. Typical. First kills are always that way." He looked her in the eye. "You killed someone last night. A human. You fed on him. In Carnegie Hall."

Caitlin felt her world spinning. She could hardly believe she was capable of harming anyone, yet somehow, deep down, she felt it was true. She was afraid to ask who it was. Could it have been Jonah?

As if reading her mind, Caleb added, "The vocalist."

Caitlin could hardly take it all in. It felt too surreal. She felt like she had just been branded with a black mark that she could never undo. She felt awful. And out of control.

"Why did I do it?" she asked.

"You needed to feed," he answered. "Why you did it *there*, and *then*, that is what no one knows. That is what started this war. You were in another coven's territory. A very powerful coven."

"So, was I just in the wrong place at the wrong time?"

He sighed, "I don't know. There may be more to it than that."

She looked at him. "What do you mean?"

"Maybe you were *meant* to be there. Maybe it was your destiny."

She thought. She thought hard, afraid to ask the next question. Finally, she summoned her courage. "So does that mean…I am a vampire?"

He turned away. After several seconds, he finally said, "I don't know."

He turned and looked at her.

"You are not a *true* vampire. But you are not a true human, either. You are somewhere in between."

"A half-breed?" she asked.

"That's what they would call it. I am not so sure."

"What is it, exactly?"

"It is a vampire who is born into it. It is against our law, our doctrine, for a vampire to breed with a human. Sometimes, though, a rogue vampire will do so. If the human should give birth, the result will be a half-breed. Not quite human, not quite vampire. It is very much looked down upon in our race. The penalty for interbreeding with a human is death. No exceptions. And the child is considered an outcast."

"But I thought you said that your Messiah will be a half breed? How can they look down on a half-breed it if will be their savior?"

"Such is the paradox of our religion," he answered.

"Tell me more," she prodded. "How exactly is a half-breed different?"

"True vampires feed from the moment they are turned. Half breeds usually don't begin to feed until they come of age."

She was afraid to ask the next question.

"When is that?"

"18."

Caitlin thought hard. It was starting to make sense. She had just turned 18. And her cravings had just begun.

"Half-breeds are also mortal," Caleb continued. "They can die, like regular humans. We, on the other hand, cannot.

"In order to be a true vampire, one would have to be turned by a true vampire, one who fed with the intent. Vampires are not allowed to turn just anyone—it would inflate our race too greatly. They must receive permission in advance from the Master Council."

Caitlin furrowed her brow, trying to take it all in.

"You have some of our qualities, but not all. And since you are not a full breed, unfortunately, the vampire race will not accept you. Every vampire belongs to a coven. It is too dangerous not to. Normally, I could petition to accept you in our ranks. But given that you are mixed…they would never allow it. No coven will."

Caitlin thought hard. If there was anything worse than finding out that she was something other than human, it was finding out that she wasn't *truly* something. Finding out that she couldn't belong anywhere. She was neither here nor there, stuck between two worlds.

"So then what was all this talk about the Messiah? About me being…*The One?*"

"Our doctrine, our ancient law, tells us that one day a messenger, a Messiah, will arrive, and lead us to the lost sword. It tells us that on that day, war will begin, a final, all-out war between the vampire races, a war which will even drag in the human race. It is our version of the Apocalypse. The only thing that can stop it, that can save us all, is this missing sword. And the only person that can lead us to that is the Messiah.

"When I witnessed what happened to you tonight, I felt certain that it was you. I have never seen any other vampire immune to such holy water."

She looked up at him.

"And now?" she asked.

He looked off into the horizon.

"I am not so sure."

Caitlin stared at him. She felt a desperation welling up.

"So," she asked, afraid for the answer, "is that the only reason you saved me? Because you thought I would lead you to some missing sword?"

Caleb stared back, and she could see the confusion in his face.

"What other reason would there be?" he answered.

She felt the wind sucked out of her, as if she had been hit by a bat. All the love that she had felt for him, the connection she thought *they* had, went rushing out in a single breath. She felt like crying. She wanted *to* turn and run, but didn't know where to go. She felt ashamed.

"Well," she *said*, fighting back tears, "at least your *wife* will be happy to know that you *were* just doing your job. That you don't have any feelings for anyone else. Or *for* anything but some stupid sword."

She turned and walked away. *She* didn't know where she was going, but she had to get away from him. *Her* feelings were just too overwhelming. She didn't know how to make sense *of* them.

She had only gone a few feet when she felt a hand on *her* arm. He turned her back around. He stood there, looking down into her *eyes.*

"She's not my wife," he said softly. "We were married once, yes, but that was 700 years ago. It only lasted a year. In the vampire race, unfortunately, they don't forget things easily. There are no annulments."

Caitlin tossed his hand off of her, "Well, whatever she is, she'll be happy to have you back."

Caitlin kept walking, right for the steps.

Again he stopped her, this time getting around her and standing directly in her path.

"I don't know how I've offended you," he said, "but whatever I did, I am sorry."

It's what you *didn't* do, Caitlin wanted to say. It's that you *didn't* care, that you *don't* really love me. That I was just an object, a means to an end. Just like every guy I've ever known. I had thought that this time, maybe, it was different.

But she didn't say that, instead, she just lowered her head, and did her best to suppress a tear. She couldn't, though. She felt the hot tears streaming down her cheeks. There was a hand on her chin, and he raised it, forcing her to look up at him.

"I am sorry," he said finally, sounding sincere. "You were right. It was not the only reason I saved you." He took a deep breath. "I do feel something for you."

Caitlin felt her heart swell.

"But you must understand, it is forbidden. The laws are very strict on this. A vampire can never, *ever*, be with a human, or a half breed, or anyone who is not a true vampire. The punishment would be death. There is no way around it."

Caleb looked down.

"So, you see," he finally continued, "if I were to feel something for you, if I were to act for some motive other than for the general good, then it would mean my death."

"So, then, what's to become of me?" she asked. She looked around, "Clearly, I'm not welcome here. Where am I supposed to go?"

Caleb looked down, shaking his head.

"I can't go home," she added. "I have no home left. The cops are looking for me. So are these evil vampires. What am I supposed to do? Go out there on my own? I don't even know what I am anymore."

"I wish I had the answer. I tried. I really did. But there is nothing more I can do. One cannot defy the Council. It would mean both of our deaths. I am sentenced to 50 years confinement. I cannot leave these grounds. If I did, I would be banished from my clan forever. You must understand."

Caitlin turned to go, but again he spun her around.

"You *must* understand! You are merely human. Your life will end in 80 years. But for me, it's *thousands*. Your suffering is short. Mine is endless. I can*not* be banished for eternity. My coven is all that I have. I love you. I feel something for you. Something even *I* don't understand. Something I've never felt with anyone in 3,000 years. But I cannot risk leaving these walls."

"So," she said, "I'll ask you again. What's to come of me?"

He just looked down.

"I see," she answered. "I'm not your problem anymore."

Caleb opened his mouth to speak, but this time she was gone. Really gone.

She made her way quickly across the terrace, and down the stone staircase. This time she was really gone, heading into the Bronx in the dark, New York City night. She had never felt more alone.

Fourteen

Kyle walked straight down the stone corridor, flanked by a small entourage of vampires. They headed quickly down the hall, their footsteps echoing, one of his aides holding a torch out in front.

They were heading deep into the corridor of command, a subterranean chamber which no vampire ever entered unless given permission. Kyle had never been down this deep before. But on this day, he was summoned by the supreme leader himself. It must have been serious. In 4,000 years, Kyle had never been summoned. But he had heard of others who had. They had gone down there, and had not come back up.

Kyle swallowed hard, and walked faster. He had always believed that it was best to greet bad news quickly, and get it over with.

They came to a large, open door, guarded by several vampires, who stared coldly back. Finally, they stepped aside and opened the door. But after Kyle passed, they held out their staffs, preventing his entourage from following. Kyle felt the door slam behind.

Kyle saw dozens of vampires lined up, at attention, along the wall, standing quietly on either side of the room. Front and center in the room, seated in a massive, metal chair was Rexus, his supreme leader.

Kyle took several steps forward and bowed his head, waiting to be addressed.

Rexus stared back with his cold, hard, icy blue eyes.

"Tell me everything you know about this human, or half-breed, or whatever she is," he began. "And about this spy. How did he infiltrate our ranks?"

Kyle took a deep breath, and began.

"We don't know much about the girl," he said. "We have no idea why the holy water did not affect her. But we do know that she was the one who attacked the singer. We have him in custody now, and as soon as he recovers, we expect him to lead us to her. He was turned by her. He has her scent in his blood."

"What coven does she belong to?" Rexus asked.

Kyle shuffled in the darkness, choosing his words carefully.

"We think she is just a rogue vampire."

"*Think!*? Do you *know* anything?"

Kyle, rebuked, felt his cheeks redden.

"So you brought her into our midst without knowing a thing about her," Rexus said. "You endangered our entire coven."

"I brought her in to interrogate her. I had no idea she would be immune—"

"And what of the spy?" Rexus asked, cutting him off.

Kyle swallowed.

"Caleb. We brought him in 200 years ago. He had proved his loyalty many times. We never had any reason to suspect him."

"Who had recruited him?" Rexus asked.

Kyle paused. He swallowed hard.

"I did."

"So," Rexus said. "Once again, you allowed a threat into our ranks."

Rexus glared back. It wasn't a question. It was a statement. And filled with condemnation.

"I am sorry, master," Kyle said, bowing his head. "But in my defense, no one here, not one vampire, ever suspected Caleb. On many occasions —"

Rexus raised his hand.

Kyle stopped.

"You have forced me to initiate the war. I will now have to re-direct all of our resources. Our master plan will have to be put on hold."

"I am sorry, master. I will do whatever I can to find them, and to make them pay."

"I'm afraid it's too late for that."

Kyle swallowed hard, bracing himself for what might come next. If it was death, he was prepared.

"I am no longer the one you need to answer to. I myself have been summoned. By the Supreme Council."

Kyle's eyes open wide. He had heard rumors all his life of the Supreme Council, the governing body of vampires who even the supreme leader had to answer to. And now he knew that it was real, and that they were summoning him. He swallowed hard.

"They are very unhappy with what went on here today. They want answers. You will explain the mistake you made, why she escaped, why a spy infiltrated our ranks, and our plans for purging other spies. You will then accept their judgment in sentence."

Kyle slowly nodded, terrified for what would come. None of it sounded good.

"We meet at the next new moon. That gives you time. In the meantime, I suggest you find this half-breed. If you can, it may just save your life."

"I promise, my master, I will summon every one of our vampires. And I will lead the charge myself. We will find her. And I will make her pay."

Fifteen

Jonah sat in the police station, very afraid. One on side of him sat his Dad, looking more nervous than Jonah had ever seen him, and on the other, his newly-hired lawyer. Across from them, in the small, bright, interrogation, sat five police detectives. Behind them stood five more, all pacing and agitated.

It was the biggest news story of the day. Not only had an internationally-acclaimed vocalist been murdered, right during his debut performance, right in Carnegie Hall—not only had he been murdered in a suspicious way, but things had managed to get even worse. When the police followed up on the only lead they had, when they had visited her apartment, four policemen were killed. To say that things had escalated was to put it mildly.

Now, not only were they after the "Beethoven Butcher" (or "Carnegie Hall Killer," as some papers were calling her) but they were also after a cop killer. A four-cop killer. Every cop in the city was on the case, and no one would rest until it was solved.

And the only lead they had was sitting across the table from them. Jonah. Her guest for the evening.

Jonah sat wide-eyed, feeling the drops of sweat forming again on his forehead. This was his seventh hour in the room. During the first three hours he had continuously wiped the sweat from his hairline. Now he just let the sweat trickle down the side of his face. He slumped in his chair, defeated.

He just didn't know what else to add. Cop after cop had entered the room, all asking the same questions. All variations on a theme. He had no answers. He couldn't understand why they kept asking him the same thing, over and over. *How long have you known her? Why did you bring her to this event? Why did she leave at intermission? Why didn't you follow her?*

How had it all come to his? She had showed up looking so beautiful. She was so sweet. He loved being with her, and talking to her. He was sure it was going to be a dream date.

Then she had started acting strangely. Shortly after the music began, he had felt a restlessness building in her. She had seemed...sick wasn't the word. She had seemed...antsy. More than that: she had seemed like she was going to burst out of her skin. Like she had to get somewhere, and get somewhere fast.

At first he had thought it was just because she wasn't liking the concert. He had wondered if taking her there was a bad idea. Then he'd wondered if maybe she just didn't like him. But then it seemed to grow more intense, and he could almost feel the heat radiating out of her skin. He had then started to wonder if maybe she had some kind of sickness, maybe food poisoning.

When she actually burst out of the place, he'd wondered if she was running to the bathroom. He was puzzled, but he waited patiently by the doors, assuming she would come back after intermission. But after fifteen minutes, after the final bell rang, he had gone back to his seat alone, confused.

After another 15 minutes had gone by, the lights in the entire room had been raised. A man had come on stage and made an announcement that the concert would not continue. That refunds would be issued. He did not say why. The entire crowd had gasped, annoyed, but mostly puzzled. Jonah had been attending concerts his entire life, and had never seen one stopped at intermission. Had the vocalist taken sick?

"Jonah?" The detective snapped.

Jonah looked up at her, startled.

The detective stared back down angrily. Grace was her name. She was the toughest cop he had ever met. And she was relentless.

"Did you not hear what I just asked you?"

Jonas shook his head.

"I want you to tell me again everything that you know about her," she said "Tell me again how you met."

"I've answered that question a million times already," Jonah answered, frustrated.

"I want to hear it again."

"I met her in class. She was new. I gave her my seat."

"Then what?"

"We got to talking a little bit, saw each other in the cafeteria. I asked her out. She said yes."

"That was it?" The detective asked. "There are absolutely no other details, not one other thing to add?"

Jonah debated with himself over how much to tell them. Of course, there was more. There was his getting beat up by those bullies. There was her journal, lying mysteriously beside him. His suspicion that she had been there. That she had helped him. That she had even beat up those guys somehow. How, he had no idea.

But what was he supposed to tell these cops? That he had gotten himself beat up? That he thinks he remembered seeing her there? That he thinks he remembered seeing her beat up four guys twice her size? None of it made any sense, not even to him. It certainly wouldn't make sense to them. They would just think he was lying, making stuff up. They were out for her. And he wasn't going to help.

Despite everything, he felt protective of her. He couldn't really understand what had happened. A part of him didn't believe it, didn't want to believe it. Had she really killed that vocalist? Why? Were there really two holes in his neck, like the newspapers said? Had she bit him? Was she some kind of…

"Jonah," Grace snapped. "I said, is there anything else?"

The detective stared down at him.

"No," he said, finally. He hoped she couldn't tell he was lying.

A new detective stepped forward. He leaned over, stared right into Jonah's eyes. "Did anything she say that night indicate that she was mentally unstable?"

Jonah furrowed his brows.

"You mean, crazy? Why would I think that? She was great company. I really like her. She's smart, and nice. I like talking to her."

"Exactly what did you talk about?" It was that female detective again.

"Beethoven," Jonah answered.

The detectives looked at each other. By the confused, unpleasant expression on their faces, one would have imagined he had said "pornography."

"Beethoven?" one of the detectives, a beefy guy in his 50s, asked, in a mocking voice.

Jonah was exhausted, and felt like mocking him back.

"He's a composer," Jonah said.

"I know who Beethoven is, you little punk," the detective snapped.

Another detective, a beefy man in his 60s with large, red cheeks, took three steps forward, put his meaty palms on the table, and leaned in close enough so that Jonas could smell his bad coffee breath. "Look pal, this isn't a game. Four cops are dead because of your little girlfriend," he said. "Now we know that *you* know where she's hiding," he said. "You better start opening up and –"

Jonah's lawyer held up his hand. "That is conjecture, detective. You cannot accuse my client of–"

"I don't give a damn about your client!" the detective screamed back.

A tense silence fell over the room.

Suddenly, the door opened, and in walked another detective, wearing latex gloves. He carried Jonah's phone in one hand, and placed it on the table next to him. Jonah was happy to see it back.

"Anything?" one of the cops asked.

The cop with the gloves took them off and threw them in the wastebasket. He shook his head.

"Nothing. The kid's phone is clean. He got a few texts from her before the show, but that was it. We tried her number. Dead. We're pulling all her phone records now. Anyway, he's telling the truth. Before yesterday, she'd never called or texted him once."

"I told you," Jonah snapped back at the cops.

"Detectives, are we through here?" Jonah's lawyer asked.

The detectives turned and looked at each other.

"My client has committed no crime, and done nothing wrong. He has cooperated entirely with this investigation, answering all of your questions. He has no intention of leaving the state, or even the city. He is available for questioning any time. I ask now that he be excused. He is a student, and he does have school in the morning." The lawyer looked down at his watch. "It is almost 1 AM, gentlemen."

At just that moment, a loud bell rang in the room, accompanied by a strong vibration. All eyes in the room suddenly turned to Jonah's phone, sitting there on the metal table. It vibrated again, and lit up.

Before Jonah could reach for it, he saw who it was from. As did everyone else in the room.

It was from Caitlin.

She wanted to know where he was.

Sixteen

Caitlin checked her phone again. It was 1 AM, and she had just texted Jonah. No response. He was probably asleep. Or if awake, he probably wouldn't even want to hear from her. But it was the only thing that she could think of doing.

As she walked away from the Cloisters, in the fresh, night air, her head started to clear. The further she got from that place, the better she felt. Caleb's presence, his energy, slowly lifted from her, and she began to feel like she could think clearly again.

When she had been with him, for some reason she'd been unable to think clearly for herself. His presence had been all-consuming. She'd found it impossible to think of anything, or anyone, else.

Now that she was on her own again, and away from him, thoughts of Jonah flooded back to her. She felt guilty for liking Caleb at all—felt like somehow she had betrayed Jonah. Jonah had been so kind to her in school, so good to her on their date. She wondered how he felt about her now, running out like that. He probably hated her.

She walked through Fort Tryon park, and checked her phone again. Luckily, it was a tiny phone, and she had hidden it well in the tiny, inside pocket of her tight dress. Somehow, it has survived through all this.

But the battery had not. It had been almost two days without charging, and as she looked down, she saw it was redlining. There were only a few minutes left before it died completely. She hoped that Jonah would answer her before then. If not, she'd have no way left to reach him.

Was he sleeping? Was he ignoring her? She couldn't blame him. She would have ignored her, too.

Caitlin walked and walked, through the park. She had no idea where she was heading. All she knew was that she needed to get far away from that place. From Caleb. From vampires. From all of this. She just wanted her normal life back. In the back of her mind, she thought that, if she walked far enough, and long enough, maybe all of this would just disappear. Maybe the rising sun would bring a new day, and this would all be washed away as a bad, bad dream.

She checked her phone. It was flashing now, almost completely dead. She knew from experience that she had about 30 seconds until it was done. She stared at it the entire time it flashed, hoping, praying, the *Jonah* would respond. That he would suddenly call and say, *Where are you? I'll come right away.* That he would rescue her from all of this.

But as she watched, it suddenly went black. Dead. Completely dead.

She tucked the phone back into her pocket, resigned. Resigned to her new life. Resigned to having no one left. She would just have to rely on herself, Like she had always done.

She exited Fort Tryon Park, and was in the Bronx, back on the city grid. It gave her a sense of normalcy. Of direction. She didn't know exactly where to go, but Joe liked that she was heading towards Midtown.

Yes. That was where she would go. Penn Station. She would catch a train, get far away from all this. Maybe go back to her previous town. Maybe her brother would still be there. She could start over again. Act as if all of this had never happened.

She looked around: graffiti everywhere, hustlers on every corner. But somehow, this time, they left her alone. Maybe they realized that she was at the end of her rope. That there was nothing left to take from her.

She saw a sign. 186th Street. It would be a far walk. 150 blocks to Penn Station. It would take all night. But that was what she wanted. To clear her head. Of Caleb, of Jonah. Of the events of the last two nights.

She saw another future ahead of her, and she was ready to walk all night.

Seventeen

When Caitlin woke, it was morning. She could feel more than see the sunlight striking her, and she groggily raised her head to get her bearings. She felt cold stone touching the skin of her arms and forehead. Where was she?

As she raised her head and looked around, she realized she was in Central Park. She remembered now that she had stopped along the way, sometime during the night, to take a rest. She had been so tired, so weary. She must have fallen asleep sitting up, leaning over and resting her arms and head on the marble railing.

It was already mid-morning, and people streamed through the park. One lady, with her young daughter, walked by and gave her a strange look. She pulled her daughter close as they passed.

Caitlin sat up straighter, and looked around. A few people stared at her, and she wondered what they must have thought. She looked down at her dirty clothes. They were covered in grime. At this point, she didn't really care. She just wanted to get out this city, this place which she associated with everything going wrong.

Then it hit her. Hunger. A pang struck, and she felt hungrier than she ever had. But it wasn't a normal hunger. It was an insane, primal urge. To feed. Like she had felt in Carnegie Hall.

A small boy playing with a soccer ball, no older than six, kicked it, by accident, right near her. He came running over towards her. His parents were far ahead, at least 30 feet.

Now was her chance. Every bone in her body screamed to feed. She stared at his neck, zoomed in on the pulsing blood. She could feel it. Almost smell it. She wanted her to pounce.

But somewhere, some part of her stopped herself. She knew that she would starve if she didn't feed, and that she would die shortly. But she would rather die than harm him. She let him go.

The sunlight was bad, but bearable. Was that because she was a half-breed? How would it have affected other vampires? Maybe this gave her some kind of edge.

She looked around, blinking at the harsh sunlight, and felt dazed and confused. There were so many people. So much commotion. Why had she stopped here. Where had she been going? Yes... Penn Station.

She felt the pain in her weary feet, sore from all the walking. But she wasn't far now. Not more than 30 blocks. She would walk the rest of the way, catch a train, and get the hell out of here. She would urge herself, out of sheer will, to become normal again. If she got far enough from the city, maybe, just maybe that would happen.

Caitlin stood slowly, preparing to walk.

"Freeze!" a voice screamed.

"Don't you move!" yelled another voice.

Caitlin turned slowly.

Before her were at least a dozen uniformed New York police officers, all with guns drawn and pointed. They kept their distance, about 15 feet away, as if afraid to get any closer. As if she were some sort of wild animal.

She looked back at them, and strangely, was unafraid. Instead, she felt a strange sort of peace rise within her. She was beginning to feel stronger than the humans. And with every passing moment, she felt less and less a part of their race. She felt a strange sort of invincibility, felt that, no matter how many of them there were, or what weaponry they had, she could outrun them, or outfight them.

On the other hand, she felt tired. Resigned. A part of her really didn't want to run anymore. From the cops. From vampires. She didn't know where she was running to, or really what she was running from. In some weird way, she would welcome being hauled off by the police. Getting arrested would at least be something normal, rational. Maybe they would shake her up and make her realize that she was just human after all.

The officers slowly, warily approached her, guns drawn, moving with the utmost caution.

She watched them come closer, more interested than afraid. Her senses had heightened. She noticed every tiny detail. The detailed shape of their guns, the contour of the triggers, even how long their fingernails were.

"Get those hands up where can see them!" a cop screamed.

The closest cops were only feet away.

She wondered what her life would have been like. If her father had never left. If they had never moved. If she'd had a different Mom. If they'd stayed put in one of the towns. If she'd had a boyfriend. Would she have ever had been normal? Would life have ever been normal?

The closest cop was now only a foot away.

"Turn around and place your hands behind your back," said the cop. "Slowly."

She slowly lowered her arms, turned, and placed her arms behind her back. She could feel the cop grab her tightly around one wrist, then the other, jerking her arms behind her too roughly, too high, using unnecessary force. How petty. She felt the cold clasp of the handcuffs, and could feel the metal cut into her skin.

The cop grabbed her by the back of head, squeezed her hair, way too tight, and leaned in close, putting his mouth beside her ear. He whispered, "You're going to fry."

And then it happened.

Before she knew what was happening, there was a sickening noise of crunching bone, followed by the splatter of blood—and the feel and smell of warm blood all over her face.

She heard shouting, and screaming, and then shots fired, all in the fraction of a second. It wasn't until she instinctively dropped to her knees and hit the ground, spun around and looked up, that she realized what was happening.

The cop who had cuffed her was dead, decapitated, his head severed in half. The other cops were firing wildly, but they were outmatched. A mob of vampires – the same ones from City Hall – had descended. They were tearing the cops to pieces.

The cops managed to shoot some of them, but it didn't do any good. They kept on charging. It was a bloodbath.

Within a matter of seconds, the cops were torn to pieces.

Caitlin suddenly felt the warm, familiar rush through her blood, felt the power filling her, rising up from her feet, through her arms and shoulders. She reached back and snapped the handcuffs clean. She brought her hands in front of her and stared, shocked at her own strength. The metal dangled on each wrist, but her hands were now free.

She jumped to her feet, watching with fascination the grisly scene in front of her. The entire mob of vampires hunched over the cops' bodies. They seemed too distracted to notice her. She realized she needed to escape. Fast.

But just before she could finish the thought, she felt an icy, super strong grip on the back of her neck. She looked over and recognize the face. It was Kyle. And he had the look of death.

He grinned at her, more of a snarl.

"We are not saving you," said. "We are simply taking what is ours."

She tried to resist. She swung her arm around but he blocked it easily and grasped her by the throat. She was losing air. She was simply no match for him.

"You may be immune to some things," he said, "but you are not nearly as strong as I. Nor will you ever be."

At that moment there was another blur of motion, and Caitlin could suddenly breathe again. She was shocked to see Kyle suddenly stumbling backwards. He went hurling back with such force that he smashed backwards into the marble railing, shattering it, and went flying over its side.

She looked over and saw what had done it.

Caleb.

He was here.

Before she could even process what was happening, Caitlin felt his familiar, tight grip around her waist, his muscled arm and torso, and felt herself being held by him as they ran and ran, faster and faster, just as they had the night before. They ran through Central Park, heading south, and in moments, the trees became a blur. They lifted into the air. Once again, they were flying.

They were up in the air, over the city, when Caleb spread his wings and wrapped them around her.

"I thought you couldn't leave," Caitlin finally said.

"I can't," Caleb said.

"So…does that mean you'll be—"

"Banished. Yes."

She felt overcome with emotion. He had given it all up for her.

As they flew, higher and higher, almost into the clouds, Caitlin had no idea where they were going. She looked down and could see that they were leaving the city. She relaxed. She was so happy to be away from it all, so ready for a fresh start. Most of all, she was happy to be in Caleb's arms. The sky before them broke into a soft orange glow, and she only wished that this moment would never end.

NOW AVAILABLE!

LOVED
(Book #2 in the Vampire Journals)

Book #2 in the #1 Bestselling series The Vampire Journals!

In LOVED (Book #2 in the Vampire Journals), Caitlin and Caleb embark together on their quest to find the one object that can stop the imminent vampire and human war: the lost sword. An object of vampire lore, there is grave doubt over whether it even exists.

If there is any hope of finding it, they must first trace Caitlin's ancestry. Is she really the One? Their search begins with their finding Caitlin's father. Who was he? Why did he abandon her? As Caitlin search broadens, she is shocked by what she discovers about who she really is.

But they are not the only ones searching for the ancient sword. The Blacktide Coven wants it, too, and they are close on Caitlin and Caleb's trail. Worse, Caitlin's little brother, Sam, remains obsessed with finding his Dad. But Sam finds himself in way over his head, smack in the middle of a vampire war. Will he jeopardize their search?

Caitlin and Caleb's journey takes them on a whirlwind of historic locations—from the Hudson Valley, to Salem, to the heart of historic Boston—the very spot where witches were once hung on the hill of Boston Common. Why are these locations so important to the vampire race? Will it lead them to the ancient sword?

But they may not even make it. Caitlin and Caleb's love for each other is blossoming. And their forbidden romance may just destroy everything they've set out to achieve….

LOVED is quite a bit longer than TURNED (at 51,000 words).

About Morgan Rice

Morgan is author of the #1 Bestselling THE SORCERER'S RING, a new epic fantasy series, currently comprising eleven books and counting, which has been translated into five languages. The newest title, A REIGN OF STEEL (#11) is now available!

Morgan Rice is also author of the #1 Bestselling series THE VAMPIRE JOURNALS, comprising ten books (and counting), which has been translated into six languages. Book #1 in the series, TURNED, is now available as a FREE download!

Morgan is also author of the #1 Bestselling ARENA ONE and ARENA TWO, the first two books in THE SURVIVAL TRILOGY, a post-apocalyptic action thriller set in the future.

Among Morgan's many influences are Suzanne Collins, Anne Rice and Stephenie Meyer, along with classics like Shakespeare and the Bible. Morgan lives in New York City.

Please visit www.morganricebooks.com to get exclusive news, get a free book, contact Morgan, and find links to stay in touch with Morgan via Facebook, Twitter, Goodreads, the blog, and a whole bunch of other places. Morgan loves to hear from you, so don't be shy and check back often!

Books by Morgan Rice

THE SORCERER'S RING
A QUEST OF HEROES (BOOK #1)
A MARCH OF KINGS (BOOK #2)
A FATE OF DRAGONS (BOOK #3)
A CRY OF HONOR (BOOK #4)
A VOW OF GLORY (BOOK #5)
A CHARGE OF VALOR (BOOK #6)
A RITE OF SWORDS (BOOK #7)
A GRANT OF ARMS (BOOK #8)
A SKY OF SPELLS (BOOK #9)
A SEA OF SHIELDS (BOOK #10)
A REIGN OF STEEL (BOOK #11)

THE SURVIVAL TRILOGY
ARENA ONE (Book #1)
ARENA TWO (Book #2)

the Vampire Journals
turned (book #1)
loved (book #2)
betrayed (book #3)
destined (book #4)
desired (book #5)
betrothed (book #6)
vowed (book #7)
found (book #8)
resurrected (book #9)
craved (book #10)

xX BabyGirlXx Gaming.

Lightning Source UK Ltd.
Milton Keynes UK
UKHW011258270520
363925UK00007B/2253

9 781939 416308